# IN SEARCH OF LOVE

Robert was there, holding out his arms and she moved into them gladly.

They had danced together before but this was different. Now they sensed something they had not known nor even suspected.

"You are beautiful, Vanda," he sighed. "More beautiful than any woman here."

She smiled.

"Are you making fun of me?"

"Why should you think so?"

"Because you have never paid me compliments before."

"Times change," he said seriously. "People change."

She could think of nothing but how it felt to be close to him. She wanted him to draw her even closer, to take her into his arms and kiss her.

Looking up, she met his eyes and was swept by an overwhelming conviction that he felt the same.

Suddenly his arms tightened about her and she felt herself being danced out of the tall windows into the garden.

# THE BARBARA CARTLAND PINK COLLECTION

Titles in this series

1.   The Cross of Love
2.   Love in the Highlands
3.   Love Finds the Way
4.   The Castle of Love
5.   Love is Triumphant
6.   Stars in the Sky
7.   The Ship of Love
8.   A Dangerous Disguise
9.   Love Became Theirs
10.  Love drives in
11.  Sailing to Love
12.  The Star of Love
13.  Music is the Soul of Love
14.  Love in the East
15.  Theirs to Eternity
16.  A Paradise on Earth
17.  Love Wins in Berlin
18.  In Search of Love

# IN SEARCH OF LOVE

# BARBARA CARTLAND

Barbaracartland.com Ltd

Printed and bound in Great Britain by CLE Print Ltd,
St Ives, Cambridgeshire

# THE BARBARA CARTLAND PINK COLLECTION

Barbara Cartland was the most prolific bestselling author in the history of the world. She was frequently in the Guinness Book of Records for writing more books in a year than any other living author. In fact her most amazing literary feat was when her publishers asked for more Barbara Cartland romances, she doubled her output from 10 books a year to over 20 books a year, when she was 77.

She went on writing continuously at this rate for 20 years and wrote her last book at the age of 97, thus completing 400 books between the ages of 77 and 97.

Her publishers finally could not keep up with this phenomenal output, so at her death she left 160 unpublished manuscripts, something again that no other author has ever achieved.

Now the exciting news is that these 160 original unpublished Barbara Cartland books are ready for publication and they will be published by Barbaracartland.com exclusively on the internet, as the web is the best possible way to reach so many Barbara Cartland readers around the world.

The 160 books will be published monthly and will be numbered in sequence.

The series is called the Pink Collection as a tribute to Barbara Cartland whose favourite colour was pink and it became very much her trademark over the years.

The Barbara Cartland Pink Collection is published only on the internet. Log on to www.barbaracartland.com to find out how you can purchase the books monthly as they are published, and take out a subscription that will ensure that all subsequent editions are delivered to you by mail order to your home.

If you do not have access to a computer you can write for information about the Pink Collection to the following address :

Barbara Cartland.com Ltd.
Camfield Place,
Hatfield,
Hertfordshire AL9 6JE
United Kingdom.

Telephone:  + 44 (0)1707 642629
Fax:          + 44 (0)1707 663041

# THE LATE DAME BARBARA CARTLAND

Barbara Cartland who sadly died in May 2000 at the age of nearly 99 was the world's most famous romantic novelist who wrote 723 books in her lifetime with worldwide sales of over 1 billion copies and her books were translated into 36 different languages.

As well as romantic novels, she wrote historical biographies, 6 autobiographies, theatrical plays, books of advice on life, love, vitamins and cookery. She also found time to be a political speaker and television and radio personality.

She wrote her first book at the age of 21 and this was called *Jigsaw*. It became an immediate bestseller and sold 100,000 copies in hardback and was translated into 6 different languages. She wrote continuously throughout her life, writing bestsellers for an astonishing 76 years. Her books have always been immensely popular in the United States, where in 1976 her current books were at numbers 1 & 2 in the B. Dalton bestsellers list, a feat never achieved before or since by any author.

Barbara Cartland became a legend in her own lifetime and will be best remembered for her wonderful romantic novels, so loved by her millions of readers throughout the world.

Her books will always be treasured for their moral message, her pure and innocent heroines, her good looking and dashing heroes and above all her belief that the power of love is more important than anything else in everyone's life.

*"When you fall in love, you want to sing with the birds, dance with the fairies, jump over the moon. It is truly the most glorious feeling in the whole wide world."*

Barbara Cartland

# CHAPTER ONE
# 1889

The Earl of Cunningham was on the last stage of his morning ride, the one that brought him in sight of Cunningham Hall, the great house that had been in his family for years.

It had been built in the early 17th. century, receiving several additions over the next two hundred years. Now it stood, glowing, in the morning sun, beautiful, imposing and magnificent.

Robert, the sixth Earl, had possessed his title for eight years and filled his position so well that he was extremely popular with all his neighbours in this corner of Kent.

He was a man in the prime of life. In his early thirties, he boasted a strong, handsome face and deep blue eyes. His mouth was stern, but he could burst into sudden laughter that transformed him.

As he galloped towards his stables this morning, he at once noticed a carriage that he recognised as belonging to Sir Quentin Sudbury, the Lord Lieutenant of the county of Kent.

The Earl groaned.

If there was one thing he disliked, it was people who called on him before breakfast. And if there was one person he found tiresome, it was the Lord Lieutenant.

'I wonder what can be wrong today?' he asked himself, as he walked into the house.

If it was just a question of money, he supposed he

would have to pay up.  He was rich, even after finding dowries for his sisters.

Two of them were older than him and had married during his father's lifetime.  Two were twins of almost his own age and the fifth, much younger, had only married a year ago.

His father had found the possession of five daughters a financial strain.  But that was because he was wildly extravagant, always buying costly pictures and furniture.

But after his death Robert had found that many of the pictures were not what they pretended to be.  His father had not been skilled at discerning fakes and many of his 'best' buys were worthless.

He had also found that there was a great deal for him to organise on the estate itself.  Farms had been somewhat neglected.  Even the garden needed more attention and more imagination to make it as outstanding as it should be.

The same applied to the forest and the river which ran through the estate.

The Earl had sold some of his good pictures, provided for his remaining sisters, and invested the rest in reviving the estate, which his father had not cared for at all well.

At last his efforts had borne fruit.  His revenues rose until once more he was as wealthy as the Earl of Cunningham expected to be.

He could remember his pride when his Uncle James had said to him,

"If you can do all this now, what will it be like in twenty years?  What a legacy you will leave to your son!"

The Earl laughed and replied,

"I will have to produce him first."

"Well, hurry up and choose a lady.  What bride would not want to come to such home?"

"I have to be certain," the Earl said, "that she loves me and not just the house."

Uncle James had laughed.

"That is true," he agreed. "You need to be very sensible. Women like a title."

The Earl had already discovered this truth. Parents said openly that they wanted their daughter to become the Countess and to live grandly at the Hall. So far he had succeeded in keeping his distance.

But there was no chance of keeping his distance from the Lord Lieutenant, so the Earl walked sharply down the corridor which led to his sitting room.

It was a charming room with windows overlooking the garden. In one corner there was a beautiful 18th. century desk. On it stood a gold ink-pot and gold-topped pens with which his grandfather, his father and now he signed their special letters.

He had added several very valuable pictures which were his favourites. He was fond of this room, just as his father had been fond of it and his grandfather before him.

But today he was not at all pleased by the sight of Sir Quentin Sudbury waiting for him. After the Earl, he owned the largest amount of land in the county, and, as Lord Lieutenant, was continually bothering him with one request after another.

The Earl had always remained on cordial terms with Sir Quentin. He had given more or less what was expected of him, or had managed to refuse requests in such a charming way that the Lord Lieutenant had departed quite content.

Now, with difficulty, he managed to smile as he held out his hand and said,

"You are very early or perhaps I am later than usual. It has been such a delightful morning that I have maybe ridden for longer than I usually do."

"You are right, Robert," the Lord Lieutenant replied, "it is a lovely morning! I was certain you would be out riding. But I waited because I have something very particular to say to you."

"What is it you want from me?"

There was silence. The Lord Lieutenant seemed to have trouble knowing how to begin, but eventually he said,

"Ever since you have inherited this house and the grounds, you have been of great value to the county and taken your father's place in the most admirable fashion."

The Earl thanked him politely, but he was wondering what all this was leading up to. He thought that Sir Quentin was looking tired and in some ways, much older than he had looked the last time he had seen him.

Now he turned directly towards the Earl, extending his hand as if he was begging for something.

"I have come to speak about an unusual matter," he said. "In short it concerns my daughter, Vanda."

"Your daughter!" the Earl exclaimed. "What is wrong? Is she ill?"

"I am glad to say that she is not. She is extremely healthy and rides a horse as fast as you do yourself."

"That is certainly true," the Earl agreed with a smile. "I have always admired her on horseback and, what is more, I have told her she is free to ride my horses any time, even the very best. And I would not say that to any other lady. And precious few men."

"Horses are something you have in common," the Lord Lieutenant said. "That is good."

He fell silent again and seemed to have trouble knowing what to say next. But at last he began again,

"I am getting old and I want Vanda to marry someone who will take my place in her life. Someone who will look after her as I have succeeded in doing."

4

The Earl was surprised.

"You know that if she is ever in any trouble you can rely on me to be her friend and protector."

"That is what I hoped you would say," the Lord Lieutenant replied. "All I can hope for is to see her married to someone who will look after her and one day will make her happy."

"Surely you need have no worries about that," the Earl said. "She is very much admired and has many suitors."

"Hmm!" said his guest in a voice that showed all too well what he thought of these gentlemen. "Whipper snappers, all of them. That is why I have come to you for help."

"My dear sir, are you asking me to become Vanda's guardian? Or her trustee perhaps to shield her from fortune hunters?"

"Guardian?" barked the Lord Lieutenant. "Trustee? Good heavens, no, sir! I want you to become her husband."

The Earl was astounded.

For a moment he could only stare at the Lord Lieutenant as if he could not believe what he had said.

Then in a voice which did not sound like his own, he said,

"You are asking *me* – to marry Vanda?"

"Exactly! I have always been fond of you, Robert, ever since you were a small boy. I can imagine no other family I would like to see united with mine than yours. You two have been friends for years and what better than that the two of you should marry? I am convinced that you would be extremely happy."

For a moment the Earl was breathless.

He was used to ambitious parents, but nobody had been as forthright as this.

After a moment he managed to say,

"Why are you in such a hurry? She is young and has plenty of time."

"She is twenty-four and far too headstrong. I am afraid she will be tempted into marriage by someone of whom I would disapprove."

"But it is she who must approve," the Earl reminded him gently. "And I must be honest and tell you I am in no hurry to get married.

"I have seen so many of my friends making mistakes. Some have told me that they were desperately unhappy but there was nothing that they could do about it."

"I am absolutely certain you would not be unhappy with my daughter," the Lord Lieutenant replied as if that settled the matter.

There was silence. The Earl realised that he was dealing with a man of awesome stubbornness. But he could be stubborn too.

"I think that is a decision only she and I can make for ourselves. No one, not even you, can make it for us."

"But I have already told you that you are certain to be happy," the Lord Lieutenant retorted impatiently.

"I am afraid it needs more than your assurance," the Earl said curtly.

"Then tell me what else it needs. A dowry? Vanda is a wealthy young woman in her own right and she will be even more wealthy when I die."

"Thank you, but I do not need to marry for money," the Earl replied coldly.

He thought this was the most uncomfortable situation he could possibly imagine. How could he talk about the feelings of his heart to a man who could only take things literally?

He was delighted when the door opened and the butler said,

"Your Lordship's breakfast will soon be inedible and cook wants me to ask your Lordship if she should make it again for you?"

"No, of course not," the Earl replied. "I will come and have my breakfast at once."

The butler bowed and left the room leaving the door open.

The Earl turned towards the Lord Lieutenant and said,

"I will certainly think over what you have said and give you my answer. But it is something I could not possibly decide in a few minutes. In fact it will probably take me several weeks."

"If you could only understand – "

"In the meantime I must not detain you," the Earl declared desperately. "I know you have many things to attend to. In fact I believe you have a meeting in the town in half an hour. You will not wish to be late."

"I was planning on taking you with me," Sir Quentin said.

Robert suppressed his anger at this effrontery, merely saying,

"And I am planning on remaining here. Good day to you, sir."

He shook the Lord Lieutenant's hand and left the room before there was any chance of his speaking again. When he reached the dining room he closed the door firmly behind him.

He sat down at the table and the butler quickly placed his breakfast dish in front of him. The Earl's face alarmed him and he wondered what could have happened to put his Lordship in a temper.

When he was alone, the Earl gave a deep sigh as his anger evaporated into exasperation.

How could he have guessed, how could he have imagined for one moment that the Lord Lieutenant, of all people, would almost demand that he should marry his daughter?

'I have no wish at the moment, to marry anyone,' he said to himself. 'I have known Vanda ever since she was born, but never for one moment have I thought of her as my wife.'

Vanda had been at school when he first inherited the title. Since then they had been good neighbours. They had seen each other out hunting and he had often danced with her at the balls which were given in the county, especially around Christmas time. But he had never fallen in love with her.

In fact, despite their sturdy friendship they bickered constantly.

'Like brother and sister,' he thought. 'And if I do marry, I want to be wildly and passionately in love, which I am sure I could never be with *her*.'

As he ate his breakfast, he thought of the women he had been enamoured with. To be honest, the majority of them had been married already, so there was no question of him escorting any of them up the aisle.

They had mostly been as he said to himself, 'how-do-you-do and goodbye!'

There was Irene, whom he had found very attractive. In fact, she had not only made him happy, but made him feel that his life would be very empty without her.

But she was already married. Her husband was in the army and therefore seldom at home. He and Irene spent one winter seeing each other several times a week. He had become her lover secretly and made quite sure no one would uncover their secret.

Then her husband had returned home. He had inherited a house in another part of England and left the army. The Earl melted tactfully away.

Irene had certainly been very alluring and charming. But the Earl could not say now that he was unhappy that he had lost her. To tell the truth, he had been becoming rather bored with her.

There had always been other women who flattered him and were eager to fall into his arms. In the end they seemed to merge into one, so that he forgot the details of exactly how pretty one girl was or how amusing another had been.

It had all been exciting and delightful. Rather like a dream from which he woke up and then found it difficult to remember how he had felt and for whom.

Yet now, when he least expected it, the Lord Lieutenant was making a demand upon him he had never expected.

'I have no wish to be married,' he told himself. 'But if I do, I want to be absolutely certain that she is someone I will love for the rest of my life. And who will love me as long.'

But was it possible, or merely an idle dream? He was beginning to wonder.

He sighed.

'What am I to do?' he asked himself. 'What *am* I to do?'

Then inspiration struck him. He must see Vanda.

He must ask her if, somehow, by some miracle, they could find their way out of the trap which the Lord Lieutenant had set for them.

\*

Miss Vanda Sudbury was a young lady of considerable beauty, firm character and disconcerting wit. At twenty-four she had been mistress of her father's house for five years and carried such authority lightly.

Her beauty was of a special kind. She was not pretty in an elegant, feminine way, but handsome, with a pair of dark, flashing eyes. Her hair was as black as the raven's wing, giving her a mysterious, almost Latin look. At times she seemed to project a natural air of majesty that was at odds with her life as a provincial English girl.

Men commonly referred to her as a fine young woman. They did not swoon over her or offer her bouquets, but they admired her and enjoyed her company, whether on the dance floor or at the hunt.

In a ballroom she was the lightest and most debonair of dancers, her tall figure swaying gracefully in her partner's arms. On horseback she was fearless, leaping every obstacle as bravely as a man.

Many a gentleman had been heard to say that Miss Sudbury was without equal amongst the ladies, by Jove yes! But then they might shuffle their feet and confess that she frightened them a little.

Her father was a mere Knight, but his position as Lord Lieutenant, plus his considerable fortune, was enough to assure Miss Sudbury a place in Society.

No gentleman, no matter how high his title, looked down on this forthright lady. If any were so unwise, she could reduce him to nothing with a look from her splendid eyes or a flash of merciless raillery.

Despite her disadvantages, she had received several offers of marriage, not all of them from fortune hunters. Some men were genuinely attracted by the air of drama that surrounded her.

But one and all she had turned down, sometimes to her father's rage. He was ambitious for his daughter and especially himself. When she had secured an offer from a Viscount, he was in ecstasies. When she refused this offer as well, there was an explosion that caused the entire household to shudder.

All except Vanda. She shuddered for no man. But after that outburst, she refused suitors without telling her father, and forbade them, on pain of dire consequences to appeal to him over her head. It said much for her strength of personality that so far no man had been brave enough to defy her.

That morning she was alone, her father having departed on his errand, and she knew that there was a morning's hard work ahead of her.

As Lord Lieutenant, Sir Quentin was used to the people of the county bringing their problems to him. He was also used to the comfortable feeling that he could rely on his efficient daughter to act as his unofficial secretary.

Vanda breakfasted alone and settled down at the desk in the library.

"Did my father leave in good time for his meeting?" she asked the maid who brought her some coffee an hour later.

"He left early, miss, but he wasn't heading for the town. The carriage went in the other direction."

"The other – ? You mean Cunningham Hall?"

"Yes, miss."

Vanda drew a sharp breath, muttering,

"If Papa has gone where I think he has gone, I will strangle him with my bare hands."

"What, miss?"

"Nothing. This coffee is excellent."

The maid hurried away, leaving Vanda staring into the distance, while thoughts seethed in her brain.

*

As Robert rode across country to Sudbury Grange he considered Vanda dispassionately.

They had always been friends. She laughed at his jokes and was a delightful guest at luncheon or dinner.

She had a gift for getting on with people and making them laugh. Her attitude towards him had always been sensible, almost comradely. She was not demanding as other women were.

He wondered nervously if Vanda wanted to marry him. Was she even behind her father's scheme? But she had given him no sign when they had been together.

He wondered why her father had chosen him as a husband for her.

But he knew the answer.

Ambition.

Like everyone in the county, he knew of the man's wrath when his daughter had refused to marry a Viscount. How Sir Quentin would have loved to be able to take those precious steps up the social ladder.

Secretly Robert admired Vanda for refusing to marry a fool just because he was a Viscount and for standing out against her father's anger.

But he admired her spirited defiance only in theory. When he finally married, he intended to choose a woman who was more biddable and less likely to pit her will against his own.

At last he turned into the drive and moved beneath the large oak trees on either side. He rather expected to see Vanda riding, as she usually did when it was a fine day.

But there was no sign of her.

He therefore rode on to the front door of the house, which was impressive, but not as well proportioned or attractive as his own.

Even before he dismounted, a footman who was seated just inside the open door, hurried out to greet him.

"Good morning, my Lord."

The Earl recognised the footman, who was called Herbert, and had been with the family for years. He had an uneasy sensation that Herbert was looking at him in a new way, as though he knew what was happening.

'Did the whole house know?' he wondered. 'Probably, yes.'

The thought made him intensely self-conscious and for a moment he almost turned and fled.

But he had never run from an awkward situation yet, so he gritted his teeth and walked into the house.

He thought that Vanda would be in the library, because the newspapers were always taken there in the morning. So he walked straight to the library and found Vanda sitting on the sofa, with the morning newspapers spread out on her knees.

She looked up and gave a little cry of surprise when she saw him.

"Robert!" she exclaimed. "I wasn't expecting to see you here this morning."

"I came in the hope of finding you alone," he replied, walking towards her.

Moving two of the newspapers, he sat down beside her.

"If you had not been alone," he said, "I should have ridden back home immediately."

Vanda looked at him wide-eyed.

"What is wrong?" she asked. "Tell me quickly."

He was so preoccupied with his own thoughts that he did not detect a hint of nervousness in her voice.

"It is not exactly something wrong," he declared awkwardly, "but I have brought a problem to you. A problem that – according to your father – concerns us both."

Vanda looked at him.

After a long pause she said in a very low voice,

"Papa has not been talking to you about my being married?"

"He came to see me this morning," Robert replied. "What he had to say – "

He stopped, too embarrassed to go on. Now that he was here his mission seemed impossible.

There was silence for a moment.

Then Vanda asked in a small voice,

"Did Papa suggest that you and I should be married?"

"Yes, he did!" the Earl answered. "You knew all about it?"

Her sigh was part despair, part exasperation.

"I hoped and prayed that Papa would not go to you," she said sharply. "He has been nagging at me for the last week or so, but when I tried so hard to dissuade him, I hoped he would keep his wild ideas to himself."

"So you tried to dissuade him?" he asked.

Vanda stared at him.

*"Of course I did!* I hope you didn't imagine that I was behind this suggestion?"

Since that thought had crossed his mind, Robert felt himself blushing. He tried to hide it and failed. Vanda's furious eyes were on his face.

"You *did* think so," she thundered. *"How dare you!* Of all the unspeakable, insufferable – "

"That is unjust."

"I suppose you think that because you are an Earl every woman in the county is after you – "

"Most of them are," he was unwise enough to say, adding hurriedly, "but not you, I realise that."

"It is too late for an apology," she proclaimed in arctic tones.

"I did not exactly apologise – "

"Then you should have done. Your accusation was ungentlemanly and uncalled for."

"I did not make any accusation," he said, aghast. "Vanda, please – "

"I think you should call me 'Miss Sudbury'."

"But I have always called you 'Vanda'."

"You will do so no longer. From this moment, 'Miss Sudbury' is more appropriate."

"Very well, Va – Miss Sudbury. I am sorry to have offended you. I didn't mean to."

"Didn't mean – ? You didn't think it was offensive to accuse me to my face of scheming to marry you?"

He felt the hair begin to rise on his neck.

"I did no such – "

"Upon my word, sir, you have a very fine opinion of yourself."

"All I said was – "

"Let us be quite clear," she snarled, "that I have had nothing to do with this appalling idea."

The Earl felt slightly piqued. Naturally he was relieved to know that she was not heart-broken, but no man liked to hear a woman say that marriage to him was an appalling idea. However much he might agree with her.

He took a deep breath.

"Then we both find the idea appalling," he said. "To be blunt, Miss Sudbury, you are the last woman in a million that I would wish to marry."

"Splendid," she responded crisply. "*You* are the last man in ten million that *I* would wish to marry."

"So we are both agreed!" he exclaimed with a touch of desperation. "Now, could we please go back to the beginning of this conversation? And this time let us both be very, very careful what we say."

# CHAPTER TWO

"You are quite right," said Vanda, calming down. "This is a very awkward conversation and we must try not to make it more difficult than it should be."

To tell the truth she was slightly ashamed of her outburst, which had only happened because she had become horribly embarrassed.

"I think it is outrageous of Papa to have bothered you with this ridiculous idea," she said, "after I had already given him my answer."

"You made your refusal very plain, I hope?" Robert asked wryly.

"I told him that nothing on earth would prevail on me to marry you. I said I would rather go to the stake – "

"Yes, yes, I follow your meaning," he interrupted, a little testily. "There is no need to elaborate."

"I just didn't want there to be any misunderstanding."

"I assure you there is no misunderstanding," Robert asserted firmly.

"Well I am sure you don't want to marry me, so I thought it would spare you any awkwardness, if I said it first that rather than marry you I would prefer to climb to the highest – "

"Thank you, there's no need to say it again."

There was a silence. Then Vanda said in a different voice,

"I will be truthful. I told Papa that although we have been friends since childhood and I am as fond of you as if you were my brother, I certainly do not love you enough to marry you."

"That is exactly what I told him," said Robert. "You are dear to me as a sister and comrade, but I have not thought of marrying you, any more than you have of me."

"How could Papa be so tiresome?" Vanda exclaimed. "It is *so* embarrassing."

"I think it would be much more embarrassing if we were not frank with each other," Robert suggested. "As this problem concerns only you and me, surely we can find some way of making your father happy without doing anything either of us will regret?"

"You know Papa," Vanda said with a touch of bitterness. "Nothing will make him happy but getting his own way. Our feelings don't concern him."

"You do him an injustice," Robert said with a wry smile. "He kept insisting that we would be happy. He seemed a little puzzled that this assurance failed to convince me."

Vanda met his eyes and found in them a kindly humour. She choked with laughter at his irony and then they were laughing together.

"Yes, he is just like that," she agreed with a sigh. "Once he has pronounced, he considers that is the end of the matter. He is high-handed, autocratic and certain that he is always right about everything, and determined to brook no argument."

"My poor girl. However have you managed to stand up to him all this time?"

"Because I am not his daughter for nothing! The melancholy truth is that I am exactly like him."

"Come, come, you do yourself an injustice. Not *exactly,* surely?"

Vanda regarded him sulphurously, but laughed again.

"Near enough," she said. "You are quite right not to want to marry me. I would give you a terrible life."

"I don't want to marry anyone at the moment. I enjoy my life too much as it is. Of course I will have to do my duty one day, to be certain there is an heir to carry on the title when I die."

"And I suppose that I too will have to marry eventually," Vanda said. "But it must be someone whom I love with my heart and my soul, and someone who loves me in the same way."

She made a wry face.

"Perhaps it will never happen. Perhaps I will remain an old maid for the rest of my life. Very well. I would find that fate preferable to marrying the wrong man."

"Meaning me."

"Meaning any man that I do not love. I want someone whom I love so much that nothing else in the world matters."

There was something very moving in the way she spoke and Robert realised that she had translated his own thoughts into words. It was not the first time this had happened, for they were good friends and he felt that she understood him.

"Have you really never met such a man?" he asked.

Vanda shook her head.

"I live in hope," she said, "but so far I have never met a man who made me feel like that. And I have certainly never met one who felt like that about me. Or, if he did, he unaccountably failed to mention the fact."

"Perhaps you frightened him too much – being so high-handed and autocratic with all your other attractions. All right, don't hit me with that cushion!"

"You deserve it."

"Anyway, several men have wanted to marry you?"

"Oh, yes, but none of them were just right. Not even the Viscount. In fact all he had to recommend him was his title. And his grand house, of course and his vast estates, and his huge fortune. In fact, I am beginning to wonder why I *did* refuse him."

"He was an idiot," Robert reminded her solemnly. "I remember you telling me so at the time."

"Did I say that?"

"Yes. You said spending your life tied to him would be a version of purgatory, and if your father was so anxious to be related to a Viscount, he should marry him himself and see how he liked it."

"That's right, I did," Vanda said, smiling. "I would never dare to talk like that to anyone but you. People are so shocked by the things I say. I think I would be wiser to stay single."

"That is just what I often feel," he agreed. "Of course I find women attractive. But I cannot imagine one spending the rest of her life with me!"

Vanda regarded him impishly.

"Really? That's not what I have heard. The gossip says that all London is awash with women desperately trying to become Lady Cunningham."

"Exactly. Wanting to become Lady Cunningham, not wanting to be my wife. A man will love a woman entirely because she is beautiful and sweet natured and he desires nothing but her heart. A woman, on the other hand, wants to marry a man with money and a title and preferably a place at Court."

20

"Poor Robert," she said satirically. "My heart bleeds for you. Who would ever suspect you are so lonely and deprived?"

"All right, Miss Sharp-Tongue. I have already admitted that I enjoy the bachelor life. There are advantages in regarding all females with suspicion. It keeps me free from snares."

"All women?" she asked, regarding him with her head on one side.

After a moment he replied,

"All women except you. Yes, you are right. There is only one woman in the world I know I can trust absolutely and rely on not to scheme and plot to take advantage of me. And it's you. We enjoy the kind of friendship I never believed possible between a man and a woman."

"And we must not spoil that friendship by doing anything stupid like getting married," she cried.

"Indeed we must not."

"So we are agreed. But whatever are we going to do now?" Vanda asked.

"Your father will not be pleased by our decision, but if he tries to harass me I shall simply refuse to discuss the subject."

"That is all very well for you," Vanda retorted darkly. "You can keep away from him, but I cannot and you know how he goes on and on. It is not going to be pleasant listening to him complaining at me from morning to night."

"You will suffer more than I will," Robert commented, pitying her.

He was remembering how often the Lord Lieutenant had got his own way, actually forcing people into doing what he believed was right.

"We must do something," he mused, without really meaning to speak.

There was silence.  Then Vanda said,

"I am going to leave home."

"My dear girl!  And go where?"

"Anywhere," she replied firmly.

"That might prove a rather difficult destination."

"I am of age.  Quite a middle-aged spinster really.  I have my own money.  I can do as I like."

"I am afraid that a woman can never really do as she likes," Robert said sympathetically.  "In that respect it really is an unjust world."

"I cannot afford to worry about being persecuted," Vanda said in her decided tone.  "I must do what I think is right for me, whatever the world says."

"And you think running away is right for you?"

"I am not running away.  I am leaving home.  There is a big difference."

"But Miss Sudbury – "

"Why have you suddenly started to call me 'Miss Sudbury', instead of Vanda?"

"You told me to," he explained patiently.

"But that was ages ago.  Anyway, it's all different now."

Robert tore at his hair.

"I pity the man who marries you," he breathed through gritted teeth.  "You will drive him into an early grave."

"Well, as long as it isn't you," she replied heartlessly, "you need not worry."

"I begin to think it should be my duty to marry you and save some other poor fellow from a dreadful fate."

"Why on earth should you do that?" she asked, fascinated.

"Because when I arrive at the bar of Heaven, St. Peter

will show me this frail, distraught creature who was once your husband, and say to me, 'you could have saved him! You knew what she was like. Instead you allowed this poor creature go to his doom without a word.'"

"Yes," she parried with relish, "and then you will be punished for enjoying your wicked life with all those disreputable ladies, instead of yoking yourself to me and suffering like a man."

"That's right, and – what do you know about my disreputable ladies?"

"I told you before – I hear the gossip."

"Gossip about the marriage market, but you said 'disreputable ladies'."

"Yes, I did, didn't I?" she said, giving him a challenging look.

He decided that it would be safer not to pursue this probe any further.

"We are getting off the subject," he said hastily.

"What was the subject?"

"You and this absurd idea of running away."

"It's not absurd. Papa is going away next week to visit his brother in the far North. He will be gone for at least a month. As usual he is trying to tidy up everything before he leaves, including you and me."

"I don't like being tidied up," Robert observed.

"Neither do I. As soon as Papa has left, I shall go abroad. I have been planning to visit France and Italy for some time. I have learned the languages, but never found a chance to use them."

"But you cannot just go travelling alone."

"I shall not be alone. I shall have Jenny."

"Your maid is hardly an acceptable companion. Vanda, you must abandon this wild idea."

Her eyes kindled in a way he recognised as the approach of temper.

"May I remind you, sir, that you are not my husband, and have no right to give me orders!"

He ground his teeth.

"It was not an order, madam, but a friendly suggestion."

"It was an order."

"It was not."

"It was. And I do not take orders from a man to whom I have just escaped marriage by the skin of my teeth."

"On the contrary. You were never in the slightest danger. But as your friend – "

"You think you can assume an authority over me. You are mistaken. There is no way you can stop me."

"I could warn your father."

He regretted the words as soon as they were spoken. Vanda leapt to her feet, her eyes wild with betrayal.

"You would do *that*?"

"No, no, of course not. I didn't mean it, Vanda. I just cannot bear the thought of you going off into the wide blue yonder with no male protection."

"I don't need male protection."

"You do."

"I do not!"

"You do, and stop arguing, I am trying to think."

She fell silent but began to pace the room, occasionally throwing him ironic glances as he frowned with the effort.

"Well?" she asked at last. "Have you come up with a suggestion of staggering brilliance?"

"Yes," he said with an air of sudden decision. "I have.

I am coming with you. That way I won't have nightmares about your safety."

"Are you serious?"

"Perfectly. When your father returns and finds you gone, I don't want to be here. This way we will both escape."

"But can we travel together without scandal?" she breathed.

"We will be brother and sister. What could be easier?" Robert was becoming fired with enthusiasm. "And who knows? When we return one or perhaps both of us may have found the answer to our problems."

"You mean we might find the love of our life?" she asked eagerly.

"I certainly think we are more likely to find that by travelling away from here where we already know everyone."

"You are right. I will leave Papa a letter saying that I have gone to visit friends in Europe. And you can always say you are fishing in Scotland or Ireland and people will accept it as a matter of course."

"As long as he doesn't suspect that we are together," she said. "Then he would try to say that we must marry because I was compromised. But we will not allow that to happen."

Quite unexpectedly Robert laughed.

"I do not believe it," he said. "Here we are planning this outrageous trip as though it was the most natural thing in the world."

"Can we really do it?" Vanda asked.

"Of course. We will go to Paris first – "

"Paris!" Vanda sighed. "We can see the Paris Exposition. It is still on, isn't it?"

"Yes, until November."

"Then we can see everything – that tower they say is the tallest in the world – "

"The Eiffel Tower," Robert supplied.

"That's right. And there are so many other places to see – "

"We will see them all," he promised. "And then we'll live from day to day, go wherever we want and leave or stay just as we want."

Vanda gave a cry of delight.

"It's a wonderful idea. And it will be very difficult for Papa to find out exactly where we are."

"That's settled," said Robert. "I will leave now and start making my arrangements. If your father departs in two days' time, we will depart the very next day, early in the morning, before anyone is awake."

"It is the most exciting thing that has ever happened to me," Vanda said. "I feel in my heart that we will be successful. No one, not even Papa, can stop us now."

Robert laughed.

"If we are successful and I am sure we will be," he said, "I will be exceedingly grateful to the *powers-that-be* for the rest of my life."

He walked towards the door, opened it and looked back at Vanda

"One thing is very obvious," he said.

"What is that?" Vanda enquired.

"No one can say we haven't tried," he replied.

Then, as he shut the door, he heard her laugh.

*

For the next few days Robert was extremely busy, sending messages to everyone with whom he held engagements for the next few weeks.

He and Vanda made their arrangements in an exchange of notes. Her carriage would be waiting behind the rear wall where it could not be seen from the house. Robert would drive up in his own carriage. His valet and coachman would deposit his bags in Vanda's coach and then his coachman would return home with a tale of having delivered him to the nearest railway station.

Several times the Lord Lieutenant called to see him, but Robert sent messages to say that he was not at home. Only on the last day did he receive Sir Quentin, but he refused to allow him to mention the dangerous subject.

He achieved this by the simple method of talking constantly about his fishing trip to Scotland. As he babbled on and on, he realised that he was sounding slightly foolish, but anything was better than allowing Sir Quentin to speak.

At last the Lord Lieutenant gave up and departed, only saying,

"I shall call on you as soon as I return. We have many plans to make."

Robert groaned, and resolved to double the time he would be away. Sir Quentin made him feel hounded and nothing could drive him away more certainly than such a feeling.

He had felt hounded for far too long. Young women and their parents pursued him, attracted, he was sure, by his wealth and title.

He was not a vain man and so it did not occur to him to consider the likely effects of his good looks and charm. He merely assumed that their interest in him was mercenary and it had made him cynical.

He had long ago made up his mind that he would not marry unless he was very much in love with his dream Goddess, and quite certain that she was the woman who would give him the happiness that no other woman would be able to do.

He had seen so many of his friends get married and regret it as soon as they had walked up the aisle.

"I was a damn fool," one of them had said to him. "We seemed well matched to me and our parents were so anxious for the marriage that I was a bridegroom almost before I became aware of it."

"And it was a failure?" Robert had asked.

"A complete failure," his friend replied. "I found her tiresome and disagreeable with nothing in common – which, to be fair, may be as much my fault as hers."

Other men with whom he had been at school had found themselves in the same position.

One had a wife who had run off with another man and left him with two children.

It was friends like these who had made Robert swear to himself that he would never suffer as they were suffering.

He had never once met a girl who had made him feel that she could be the right wife for him.

'Perhaps now I never will,' he thought, as he made urgent preparations to escape yet one more father who was determined to force him up the aisle.

The irony of the fact that he was escaping in the company of the very daughter he was refusing to marry was not lost on him.

The Lord Lieutenant was due to leave that evening. To make sure that he had really gone, Robert allowed one of his grooms, who was sweet on a housemaid at Sudbury Grange, to have the evening off to court her. The lad returned to say that Sir Quentin had departed and to deliver a letter for the Earl.

Opening it, Robert found just one sentence written on the sheet of paper.

*I will be ready tomorrow morning at six o'clock before everyone in the house is awake.*

There was no signature, but he knew it was Vanda's handwriting.

He sent a note by return which was as brief as hers.

*Six thirty and don't be late.*

He arrived promptly next morning. Vanda met him, smiling with relief.

As her coachman started to help with the baggage she said in a voice loud enough to be heard by anyone,

"I am so glad that you're on time, because the London train leaves Maidstone at seven-fifteen."

"And I certainly don't wish to miss it," Robert replied in the same tone. "My friends in London are expecting me, as, I dare say, are yours."

"Yes, indeed," she said brightly. "Do you intend to remain in London for long before moving on?"

"A week perhaps," he replied. "Then I will be heading for Scotland and some really good fishing."

Having made sure that everyone knew they were going to London, they took their seats in the carriage. Jenny, Vanda's maid, chose to sit on the box. She had eyes for the coachman who was certainly very handsome.

"What will your father think when he finds you gone?" he whispered as they moved off.

"I left a note saying I am staying with friends. I have given the name of people who do not exist and said we might all be going abroad for a week or two."

Robert laughed.

"You are a genius, that is just what you are!" he told her. "I hope I have been as clever as you, but I doubt it."

"Never mind," she smiled kindly. "I don't suppose duplicity comes as naturally to you as it does to me."

*"Does* it come naturally to you?" he asked, slightly startled by this frank speech.

"It does to every woman. As you said yourself, the world is unjust to women. This is how we survive."

When he was silent she said,

"Now I have shocked you."

"Not really. When I think of my sisters, there isn't one of them who is capable of telling a plain fact, or confining themselves to the truth if they could think of a better fantasy."

"It's easy for you to disapprove. You are the master and can afford to be plain. A woman has to use roundabout and subtle ways."

On reflection he had to admit that she was speaking a great deal of truth.

"We ought to consider what we are going to call ourselves," Vanda suggested.

"I have thought about this. I believe I should keep my own name. It will be a lot simpler."

"Then who am I?"

"One of my sisters."

"Which one?"

"It doesn't matter," he said with a grin. "Everyone lost count of them years ago."

"Yes, I see how that could work," she mused. "Anyone who is confused about which one I am will not be able to say so."

Soon the carriage was driving into the forecourt of Maidstone Station. The coachman summoned a porter to assist them with the luggage.

"These are for the London train."

"I will go and buy the tickets," Robert said, beginning to walk into the station.

"Goodbye Cooper," Vanda said. "Hasten home."

"Hadn't I better stay and see you aboard the train, Miss Vanda?"

"That won't be necessary," she said brightly. "Goodbye, Cooper."

"I don't know, miss. It seems to me – "

*"Goodbye, Cooper."*

After what seemed like an age he drove away. Vanda and Jenny hurried into the station, to find Robert buying tickets.

"Our luggage is on its way to the Dover platform," he said. "I explained the change as soon as we were out of Cooper's sight."

"I had the greatest difficulty getting rid of him," Vanda said gloomily. "Let's hide in the waiting room until the train comes."

"Hide? Are we a pair of hiding criminals, then?"

"It feels like it. Isn't it fun?"

After a moment he was obliged to admit that it was at least a novel experience.

"How much do I owe you?" she asked as they entered the waiting room.

"Nothing."

"You cannot pay for my ticket and Jenny's. Now how much?"

Seeing the baleful look in her eyes, he hastened to tell her the amount. Vanda counted it out and thrust it forcibly into his hand in a manner that reminded him of Lady Macbeth plunging in a dagger.

"Thank you," he said meekly.

When the train reached the station, they boarded it without further incident and a couple of hours later they were steaming into Dover. Robert purchased the ferry tickets, after promising Vanda that she could pay her share and soon they were aboard.

Vanda stood eagerly at the rail, watching the bustling port, almost stamping her feet with eagerness to be gone.

"Will you be patient?" he asked her.

"No," she replied at once.

Robert laughed.

"I might have guessed you would say that."

"I suppose you find me very annoying," Vanda responded cheerfully.

"No, I am feeling very kindly towards you at the moment. I was feeling a bit bored with my life and you have found me a new adventure."

He eyed her mischievously as he added,

"It may, of course, all end in tears and recriminations."

"Never," Vanda said firmly. "Because you have been brave enough to take me on this marvellous voyage, I will always be grateful, even if at the end of our journey, I return to find that Papa has discovered another Earl or perhaps even a Duke who he would like as his son-in-law."

"Ahah! You are planning to exchange me for a Duke! Now I see the whole plot."

Looking up into his face, alive with laughter and the breeze ruffling his hair, Vanda thought that at that moment she would not exchange him for any other man on earth.

It had never occurred to her that he was so handsome.

'But he probably looks especially good to me just now,' she thought, 'because he is giving me my own way. It is just my over-bearing, high-handed nature that's giving him a halo.'

The thought made her laugh, and Robert looked at her quickly.

"What is it?" he asked.

"Nothing, I – oh, look we're moving."

They had indeed started to glide away from the quay and in another few minutes they had left the port behind.

"We are on our way," Robert said to Vanda and she laughed with joy.

"I must be dreaming," she gasped. "I expect to wake up in a moment and find myself in my own bed. But, oh, I want the dream to go on forever!"

With a sudden determined gesture, she removed her hat and pulled her hair down so that it flowed freely.

"And I want you to have whatever you want," Robert announced.

He was looking at her, but she was not looking at him. She was facing out to sea in the direction they were heading, her hair, blown by the wind, streaming out behind her.

She was no longer the sedate young lady he had always known. She might have modelled for the spirit of freedom – wild, uninhibited, eager for adventure.

From where he was standing, he could study her profile, the clean line of her forehead and nose, the generous mouth and the chin that he had often thought a little too firm for a young lady.

Now he realised how wrong he had been. What he saw in her face was strength and courage. How many women could boast these attributes or indeed her readiness to sally forth and challenge the world?

Suddenly he realised that there was no companion he would rather have beside him than this woman.

# CHAPTER THREE

At Calais they boarded the train for Paris and settled down comfortably in their seats.

As Vanda pulled off her gloves something caught Robert's attention.

"What is that on your left hand?"

She held up her hand so that he could see the two rings, one of them a gold band and the other a sparkling diamond solitaire of obvious value.

"These were my mother's," she said.

"But why are you wearing them? People will think we are married."

"Not us. Me. I was married and widowed. That will explain why there are different names on our passports, if anyone should notice."

"Ah, yes," he said. "Now you mention it, we should have thought of that. When did you marry and how long have you been a widow?"

"I haven't decided that yet."

"Then you must decide at once. It is essential for you to think yourself into your part until you believe every word of it. That's what a famous actress told me that she did and because she was such a huge success, I am sure she was right."

"I see," Vanda said slowly. "A famous actress.

Hmm." Her smile was quizzical.

"And I am not telling you who she was, so don't ask."

"But she was a huge success?"

"I have already said so."

"You two were obviously *very* close," Vanda said.

"If we were, I should not tell you."

"Was she really exciting?"

"Yes."

"Did she give you any other interesting lessons?"

"Vanda, I am warning you – "

"But you were the one who mentioned her," she said with wide-eyed innocence. "I think it's splendid that you can be so honest about the women in your past – "

"Who said she was in my past?" Robert parried before he could stop himself.

"Really? You mean she – ?"

"That's enough," he said repressively. "Can we drop the subject now?"

She glared at him.

How satisfying, he thought, to have spiked her guns.

It was late afternoon when they reached Paris and climbed out onto the platform, both slightly stiff after the long journey.

"Perhaps we won't be able to find rooms in a hotel now that the Exposition has started," Vanda said plaintively. "I suppose I should have thought about that problem."

"We will head straight for the most expensive hotel in Paris," he replied. "That will be our best chance."

Luck was with them. They arrived at the *Hotel du Mazarin* in the Champs Elysee, just as a French nobleman was leaving early, having been summoned home for a family crisis. Robert swiftly booked his suite and within a few minutes they were installed on the first floor.

When she and Jenny had finished her unpacking Vanda came to a decision, which she announced as soon as Robert came to her door.

"I need a whole new wardrobe," she proclaimed. "Immediately."

"What do you mean, immediately?" he asked in alarm.

"I mean, let's go shopping right now."

"But the shops will be closing."

"Then we will have to hurry."

In what was left of the day, she managed to buy an elegant travelling dress and an evening gown that made her sigh with delight when she saw herself in it. It was a dramatic creation in dark red velvet, trimmed with silver that outlined her bosom and narrowed in tightly to her waist, before flaring out over her hips.

She was a little concerned to discover how low it was cut in the front. But happily she remembered that she was a married woman, albeit a widowed one and she could therefore be more daring.

When Robert collected her that evening, she felt satisfaction at seeing him stare at the picture she made.

"Exactly how long have you been a widow?" he asked cautiously.

"Two years," she announced dramatically. "I have spent that time grieving in seclusion. But then you, like a good brother, told me I had mourned long enough."

"I did?"

"Of course. You said you understood that poor Charlie had been the love of my life, but he would not want me to mourn for ever. You reminded me that I am still young and it was time for me to return to the world, to dance and sing again."

"Oh, really, Vanda!" Robert exclaimed in disgust. "I would never say anything so revolting."

"Well, you said something like it, I'm sure."

He covered his eyes with his hand.

"Do you think my gown is suitable for an emerging widow?"

"It is extremely revealing," he replied slowly, trying not to feast his eyes on what it revealed. Vanda's bosom was creamily perfect and only perfection could have done justice to her gown.

"I am not a young girl, but a woman of the world," she asserted. "Poor, dear Charlie liked me to dress like this. Red was his favourite colour, you know, and he just adored me in diamonds."

She flicked her fingers in the direction of the diamond tiara on her head, from which danced two silvery feathers. More diamonds nestled about her neck.

"Vanda for Heaven's sake!"

"I am only doing what you told me, getting into the part."

"Well, if you want to play your part properly, do not give your husband a name like Charlie. It simply doesn't sound right."

"Hector," she responded at once.

"If you must."

"Dear Hector. He so loved me in red. He said to me, 'Vanda beloved, red for the setting sun and diamonds for the sparkle in your eyes.'"

"I am going to be sick," Robert declared with feeling.

"You never understood poor Hector."

"Why the devil was he 'poor Hector'? Apart from the misfortune of being married to you?"

She ignored this remark with dignity.

"You did not appreciate him."

"Maybe not, but if that's how he talked to you, I am dashed glad he's dead!"

"He used to say I was the star that guided his way, the sun that illuminated his path – "

"No really, my dear girl! You are now overdoing it."

She burst out laughing. He joined in and together, in great good humour, they walked downstairs to dinner in the hotel restaurant.

As they entered Robert was aware that heads turned to look at them. He was quite used to this reaction because of his title and importance in Society, but now he could sense something different. It was his companion who was attracting the attention.

He had often seen her in a ballroom, but never before had he known her become the object of such admiration. He guessed it had something to do with the way she was dressed. An unmarried girl could never get away with red velvet. It was a gown for an experienced woman and it suited Vanda perfectly.

'But of course,' he thought, 'she isn't a girl. She is a woman of twenty-four. Some would call her an old maid. But she is certainly not. She is simply magnificent!'

"Tell me more about Hector?" he asked when they were seated and the waiter was pouring champagne.

He made the request chiefly because he was delighted by her witty invention and wanted to hear what she would say next.

"At first he loved me from afar," Vanda told him. "We had to meet in secret."

"Why?"

"You, of course. You were totally unreasonable. You disliked him and you opposed us at every step. Finally we ran away together. In revenge you withheld my fortune – "

"I am a real tyrant, aren't I?" he said affably.

"A monster. I threw myself at your feet – "

"How did you manage that if you had run away?"

"I came back."

"Not a lot of point in going then."

"I came back when we were safely married."

"Just you? What about Hector? Wasn't he man enough to face my wrath?"

"Hector was a poet."

"Oh, God!"

Seeing that she had pushed him too far Vanda distracted his attention by saying,

"This champagne is lovely."

He refilled her glass and watched the delicious enjoyment on her face.

"Where was I?" she asked at last.

"Throwing yourself at my feet."

"Ah, yes. I clasped my hands and implored you not to be so hard hearted."

"I hope I threw a vase of water over you."

"No, you succumbed to brotherly feeling."

"Oh, I did that, did I?"

"Hector joined me – "

"Once the danger was past."

"Once he was sure of being treated with the proper respect."

"It is no longer a mystery to me why your husband died," Robert observed with a grin. "Obviously I murdered him in a moment of total exasperation!"

"Let us drink to that," Vanda said cheerfully.

They clinked glasses.

"The stage lost a fine actress in you," he added. "Or do I mean a fine dramatist, since your powers of invention seem so considerable."

"Oh, I would have loved the theatre," Vanda sighed. "Life is so dull at home. I hate being a sedate young lady."

"When were you ever sedate?" he could not resist asking.

"Well, never really," she mused, not in the least offended. "But on the outside I needed to pretend. I used to long for escape and I thought it would come in the form of a handsome Knight on a white charger.

"But when I began to receive offers they were from men who were even duller than Papa. To have accepted any of them would have meant jumping out of the frying pan into the fire. Only it would not have been as exciting as a fire. More like a pool of tepid water."

"But surely," said Robert, "some of them must have been amusing and intelligent?"

"They didn't strike me that way. All they could think of was paying me compliments and trying to kiss me."

"Most women would consider such behaviour as being amusing and intelligent in a man," he pointed out.

"Then most women have a very narrow view of life," she retorted firmly.

That was true, he realised. It was beginning to dawn on him that Vanda's view of life was more wide-ranging than he had ever encountered in any other woman.

"How did you feel about the men who tried to kiss you?"

"I did not particularly want to kiss any of them either."

"Does that mean you never did kiss one of them?" he asked and was suddenly very interested in the answer.

"Oh, I think there was one," she mused. "Or maybe

two or three. I cannot really remember."

"Cannot remember whether you kissed one man or many?" he echoed, aghast.

"Does it matter? One man is very much like another in that situation, you know."

"No, I didn't know," he replied, rather testily. "You must educate me in the matter."

"Well, they all say the same things – you are the girl of their dreams – how have they lived so long without you – they wake thinking of you and go to sleep thinking of you. You know the kind of patter."

Robert did indeed know the kind of patter, having uttered just such sentiments to his various lady loves. For the first time he wondered how the ladies had received these declarations. Had they secretly been laughing at him? Bored? Comparing him with other men?

He felt himself grow hot and cold.

"And then," Vanda continued, "they clutch you too tight and breathe wine fumes all over you. Or cigar fumes, which are even worse!"

"Of that I cannot approve," he said. "To breathe fumes over a lady is ill-mannered."

"It is something you have never done, I am sure."

"Never. I would like to believe that no lady has been given cause to complain of my behaviour."

"What, never, in the course of a colourful career?"

"My career has not been as colourful as all that," he replied untruthfully. "You don't want to believe all the gossip you hear."

"Shame! The gossip about your exploits has been my favourite entertainment for years."

"There have been, I admit, one or two ladies in my life who I thought were very attractive. But somehow, sooner or later, they disappointed me. All I wanted to do was to leave them when I realised that what I was seeking from them was just not there."

"Yes," she reflected. "That's how it is. You hope and hope, but that mysterious 'something' is always missing."

As she spoke she gave a little melancholy sigh and suddenly the atmosphere changed. Looking up, she met Robert's eye and they were no longer laughing.

"You will find it one day," he said gently. "But when you do, do not let him suspect that other men have kissed you. Every man wants the woman he marries to be his completely and not to bore him with tales of those who have been there before him."

"Bore him?" she pondered. "Yes, I see."

It crossed Robert's mind that the story of Vanda's romances would not be boring so much as infuriating, enraging, tormenting and agonising.

After a moment, he said,

"Forget it! Forget the past just as I am trying to do. Let us pretend that we have only just grown up and are stepping into a new world.

"When we were children we had vague ideas of what the future would be. Like you, I was disappointed that it was not as thrilling and adventurous as I had hoped."

"That's true," Vanda agreed. "I thought the great love of my life would appear at the first ball I attended."

He laughed.

"I thought I would fall in love with someone so beautiful that every man would be jealous of me."

"And you were disappointed?"

"Like you, I found that the members of the opposite sex were all much of a muchness. That is why I have never married. Perhaps we are asking too much. Perhaps we are

42

too romantic or unrealistic and what we want simply isn't possible."

"But that is a doctrine of despair," Vanda said. "What we are looking for is love, real true love that can thrive, even though not everyone finds it. Some people know love. Why shouldn't we?"

"I do not know, except that some are luckier than others. And sometimes I feel that I am going to be one of the unlucky ones."

Vanda nodded.

"Yes, I do know what you mean," she murmured softly.

He glanced up at her, smiling gently. Almost without realising what he was doing, he reached out and laid his hand over hers. She moved her fingers to clasp his and her smile was warm.

"Robert, dear friend, what a pleasure to see you!"

Vanda snatched her hand back and looked quickly over her shoulder to see who had spoken. She found herself looking at a tall, middle-aged man with grey hair and a ginger moustache. He was beaming with pleasure as he advanced on Robert, his hand outstretched in greeting.

"Guilbert!" he said, rising and taking his hand.

There was a flurry of greetings. The man was accompanied by a beautiful, elegant woman in her forties, who also greeted Robert as an old friend.

"When we last met, you had not succeeded to your title," remarked the man he had addressed as Guilbert. "But of course we heard the news that you were now Lord Cunningham."

Robert turned to Vanda.

"My dear, I don't think you have met my friend, Count Guilbert de Fontellac and his charming wife. My friends, this is Madame Sudbury, my sister. One of my many sisters I should say."

"But who has not heard of the fascinating Cunningham girls?" the Count replied gallantly. "How delightful to meet one of them at last."

He bowed low over her hand, before introducing Vanda to his wife.

There was one introduction left to be made. Behind him stood a man of about thirty with dark Latin good looks.

"My good friend from Italy, Piero Farnese," Guilbert said. "He is visiting us."

Piero greeted Robert with perfect courtesy, but his attention was all for Vanda. His large, chocolate brown eyes seemed to burn into hers.

The two parties joined up and arranged themselves around the table. The Count called for more champagne.

Piero made sure of securing a seat beside Vanda and the Countess, Vanda was amused to note, made sure of sitting next to Robert.

"Will your husband be joining us, Signora?" Piero asked.

"Alas, monsieur, my husband is no longer with us," she declared, sadly lowering her eyes.

"An infinite tragedy," he said at once. "Has he been dead for long?"

"For almost two years. I have spent that time in mourning and would have remained in seclusion but for my brother, who insisted that it was time for me to emerge once more into the world."

"Then your brother has been the benefactor of all men, Signora, for he has allowed your beauty to shine upon us again."

"You are too kind," she responded modestly. "I was afraid, you see, that it was improper for me, a widow, to appear in Society, no longer wearing black."

A torrent of Italian poured from him. Vanda, who had studied the language, but with no opportunity to practise it, listened intently and could translate a great many flattering things about herself.

While she seemed to devote all her attention to Piero, she managed a sideways glance that showed her that the Countess was talking intently with Robert. She heard her own name mentioned and guessed that he was telling her story, as they had worked it out together. At the same time she could see that the lady was making eyes at him.

"Of course you did not understand me," Piero said. "I shall take great pleasure in telling you again in English."

"But I did understand," Vanda said. "Some of it, anyway.

"You know my language?"

"A little, but my understanding is very poor."

"You understand *bella?*"

Vanda laughed.

"Yes, I understand that word."

"And *bellissima?*"

"That too."

He was holding her hand between both his as he launched into a speech of ardent admiration. Vanda had to try hard to suppress an impulse to giggle.

At the same time, she was enjoying herself.

The conversation became general. The Count and Countess explained that they were visiting Paris to experience the Exposition. Tomorrow they would return to their Chateau, where there was to be a grand ball in the evening.

"To which, of course, you are both invited," the Countess said.

"What do you think?" Robert asked her.

"I would love to accept," Vanda enthused.

*"Oh, grazie!"* Piero exclaimed. *"Renderai tutto meraviglioso con la tua presenza."*

"That's very kind of you," she said.

*"Danzeremo assieme tutti i balli."*

"Not every one – " she protested.

But Piero's voice rose in wild declaration.

*"Ammazzero il primo che si provera di ballare con te."*

He delivered a smacking kiss on her hand and seemed likely to continue up her arm but for Robert, who coughed loudly.

Piero seemed to return to himself as from a dream.

"He is glad that we are coming to the ball," Vanda translated, self-consciously.

"So I see," Robert said.

Piero seemed to become aware of a chill in his manner.

"You permit?" he asked, still holding Vanda's hand like a trophy. "You are not offended that I bow down in tribute to *La Signora?"*

"Is that what you're doing?" Robert muttered, just audibly.

Aloud he said,

"It is entirely a matter for my sister what she permits or does not permit. However, I think she is ready to retire. It is very late and she is tired after a long journey."

"Am I?" Vanda asked.

"Certainly you are. We shall have a busy day ahead of us tomorrow. I believe you said you wanted to see the Eiffel Tower."

"But it will be my pleasure to show you the Tower,"

Piero volunteered at once. "I will call on you early tomorrow morning."

"That will be lovely," Vanda smiled, before Robert could speak.

"And we will see you in the evening, at the ball," the Countess said.

With smiles and compliments the party broke up and Robert escorted his 'sister' to her room.

"Come inside for a moment," she said, her eyes sparkling with anger. "I have something to say to you."

"And I have something to say to you," he replied, following her inside and closing the door behind him.

Vanda turned on him, eyes flashing.

"How dare you order me to bed!" she snapped wrathfully. "I am not a child and I am not really your sister."

"That is only too evident. Any sister of mine would behave with more propriety."

"I behaved with perfect propriety."

"Well, if you call it proper for a man you have barely met to treat your hand as though it was his personal plaything – "

"He did no such thing."

"I thought he was going to detach it and take it home with him. I am very sure he would have liked to."

Vanda gave a choke of laughter and found Robert's chilly eyes on her.

"I amuse you, ma'am?" he asked austerely.

"It just sounded so funny."

"It was not intended."

"You are making far too much fuss about a trivial incident. Just because a handsome young man flirts with me – "

"Was that all he was doing? Flirting? Tell me about that little conversation you were having in Italian?"

"He said my presence at the ball would make everything lovely," Vanda recited. "I said he was too kind. He said we would dance every dance together. I said it couldn't be every dance, and he said he would kill any other man who tried to dance with me. That is all."

"All?" Robert echoed, appalled. "You have only just met him."

"Well, nobody understood the conversation."

"Thank goodness!"

Robert was at a loss to explain his own behaviour. One part of him realised why Vanda, a girl whose life had hitherto been sadly restricted, wanted to exult in her new freedom.

But the other part of him had received a nasty shock. This was not the Vanda he had thought he was accompanying. She was more exuberant, more flirtatious, and – yes, more feminine than he had ever known her.

The intimacy of their travel arrangements began to seem slightly improper. The thought had not occurred to him, but that was when he had seen her purely as a sister.

Now she was looking less like a sister every moment.

Just what she did look like was something he had yet to decide.

"You know nothing about Piero," Vanda said, "and you have no right to criticise him. Or me."

"I did not precisely criticise you – " he said lamely.

"You have accused me of behaving improperly with a man!"

"You attach too much to a few intemperate words," he replied. "Perhaps I spoke hastily – if I did I apologise. But you should behave with circumspection."

"I have behaved with circumspection for the last two years. My mourning is over. You said so yourself."

"In this fantasy world you have created I may have said so. In reality – "

"Who cares about reality?" Vanda asked with an airy gesture. "I have had enough of reality. Now I want something else and this is the only way I am ever going to get it."

"I merely ask you to be a little restrained in the liberties that you permit to men."

"May I remind you, that it is entirely a matter for your sister what she permits or does not permit? Those were your very words."

"I must have been out of my mind. I was naturally assuming that 'my sister' had some idea of decorum."

"You assumed no such thing. Besides, a widow is allowed a great deal more licence than an unmarried girl."

"But you are not a widow!"

"But the men think I am. Isn't it fun?"

He drew himself up to his full height.

"I see it is useless to speak to you," he said with dignity. "I shall retire and leave you to your own reflections."

"What a good idea," she agreed affably. "I am looking forward to my reflections."

He gave her a quelling look. But, as it entirely failed to quell her, he withdrew to his own room.

# CHAPTER FOUR

"The Paris Exposition is intended to mark the centenary of the French Revolution," Vanda recited.

She was reading aloud from a booklet she had found in her room the previous evening. She had read it from end to end, then again when she dressed and now she was reading it once more over breakfast.

She had insisted on eating the first meal of the day in the downstairs restaurant, saying that this would enable them to "watch the Parisian world go by."

Robert only wished he could stifle a feeling that she wanted to be sure of seeing Piero arrive.

"There are numerous museums and exhibitions," she continued, "but the most spectacular of all is the Eiffel Tower. Built by Gustave Eiffel, it stands three hundred metres high and is the tallest building in the world. "It is lit by ten thousand gas lamps, while two floodlights cast their beams over Paris.

"I sat at my window and watched it last night," she added, lowering the leaflet. "With all those lights twinkling in the dark, I could see it even from this distance. Oh, I just cannot wait to visit it."

"And we will visit it, just as soon as you have finished your breakfast," Robert said. "But that will take a long time since you are doing more reading than eating."

She dropped the leaflet and began to tuck in.

"Stop pretending not to care," she said. "You were looking out at the Tower too."

"I was not."

"You were. I walked out onto my balcony and I could clearly see you at your window."

"It is a great monument," he said defensively. "Naturally I take a polite interest."

Vanda gave a discreet chuckle, which he pretended not to hear.

Glancing at her a moment later he was disconcerted to see her rising from her seat, a delighted smile on her face.

Looking round, Robert saw Piero advancing, his hands outstretched to Vanda. Behind him was an extremely handsome man of about the same age.

"Signora," Piero said, taking Vanda's hands and kissing them one by one, "it is such a joy to see you again. All night I have dreamed of your beauty and I have told my friend François so much about you, that he has insisted on coming with me this morning, so that I can prove I did not exaggerate!"

François turned out to be the eldest son of Count Guilbert de Fontellac, whom they had met the previous day. He greeted Robert with deep respect.

"We met once before when you were visiting my parents," he said. "I am honoured to meet you again."

Having taken care of the courtesies, he turned and greeted Vanda effusively.

"My friend Piero cannot stop talking about this wonderful lady he has met and I too must meet her," he announced, kissing Vanda's hands as well.

Robert groaned inwardly.

The two young men pulled up chairs and joined them

at the table, both full of eagerness for the day ahead of them.

"There are so many sights to see and explore," François enthused. "And we shall so much enjoy showing them to you."

"Then perhaps we should leave now," Robert suggested.

"You do not need to come if you don't want to," Piero said quickly. "Perhaps you have old friends you would like to visit. You can leave the Signora in our capable hands with an easy mind."

Robert regarded him wryly.

"I think not," he replied.

"But there is no need to trouble you if you would rather be doing something else," Vanda said sweetly.

"But then I would miss the Eiffel Tower," he told her. "And I am *longing* to see the Eiffel Tower. I wouldn't miss it for the world. Am I making myself clear?"

"Perfectly," she said, pulling a face.

"Good." He lowered his voice and spoke close to her ear, so that his breath fanned her skin. "Because if you imagine for one moment that I am going to leave you alone with this pair of addle-pates, you are very much mistaken."

Vanda turned her head slightly so that she was looking directly into his eyes. She could still feel his warm breath, only now it was whispering against her lips. She steeled herself against such a pleasant sensation and assumed an ironic tone.

"Really?"

"Yes, really," he replied. "So remember that, madam, and *behave yourself!*"

"I am not going to get the chance to do anything else, am I?" she retorted.

"I am glad you understand that. Now, shall we go?"

"There is not a lot of point now you have spoiled all my fun."

"On the contrary, the Eiffel Tower is considered to be most instructive. You will have enormous fun climbing the steps."

She gave him a withering look, but did not risk challenging him further.

Besides, there was no need. She knew plenty of ways of getting her own back.

It was a lovely sunny day as the four of them climbed into an open carriage and drove the two miles to the Eiffel Tower. From a distance they could see it, rearing up against the sky like a beautiful spider's web.

When at last they were standing beneath the huge arch, looking up, Vanda said,

"How do we get up there?"

"We walk," Robert said. "The lifts have not opened yet."

"Most of them have not," François corrected him. "But just one is working. Follow me."

He led the way to one of the four corners where the lifts were situated and joined the queue that was waiting there. As it was quite early, the queue was still fairly short and soon the doors were opening.

Vanda watched anxiously as the lift filled up with those in front of them. At the last moment Robert took her hand and drew her quickly in. The doors shut and they were rising, leaving Piero and François behind.

"You did that on purpose!" she accused him. "Don't deny it."

"Far from denying it, I am proud of it. If I had to listen to any more from that pair of ninnies I would have done something desperate."

"There's no need to call them ninnies just because they admire me."

Robert gave her a smile that was obscurely disturbing.

"You do not need admiration from them, Vanda."

She looked up at him, her head on one side.

"I didn't say I needed it, only that I enjoy it."

"And what happens when it's time to come down to earth?"

"I don't think we will ever come down to earth," she sighed, deliberately changing his meaning and looking at the world that was swiftly falling away beneath them.

"You could be right," he said, so quietly that she could not hear him properly.

"What did you say?"

"Nothing," he said hastily. "Are you enjoying yourself?"

"Of course I am," she declared firmly.

In truth she was beginning to feel a little nervous. If she had been asked whether she was afraid of heights, she would have said that she was not, but she had never experienced height like this.

The Tower was a lattice work of steel girders, with spaces between that gave a clear view of the fast receding ground. It was like flying and nothing in her whole life had prepared her for such an experience.

Almost unconsciously she reached out and felt her hand clasped in his firm, powerful grip.

At last the lift stopped. She felt too tense to move, but he drew her gently forward, out onto the platform.

The wind took them by surprise. She gasped and swayed, feeling Robert's clasp tighten.

"It's all right," he said. "I am holding you."

"Are you sure?"

"Quite sure. Do you want to go back down?"

"No, I want to go to the edge."

"I don't think you should?"

"But it is quite safe really," she said bravely. "The rail is too high to fall over."

Still holding him she moved cautiously to the edge and looked over.

"Look at the ground," she cried. "It's so far away."

"Yes, it is magnificent, isn't it?" he agreed.

For a moment they forgot everything else and stood gazing down in wonder.

"The world looks so different from here," she exclaimed in amazement. "I never thought it could be like this."

"No, it's like being able to see for ever," he said.

She turned and smiled at him. He smiled back. In the same moment they both became aware that he was still holding her and she was still clinging on to him.

Neither of them moved. On that high breezy platform it was as though time had stopped so that the world spun around them and they remained, motionless, in the centre.

Vanda drew in a deep breath of joy. She was growing accustomed to the height and beginning to pick out details of the incredible view.

At last she turned to look at Robert to find him gazing back at her, stunned. She wanted to say something, but there was nothing to say.

"Ah, there you are! We wondered if you had both been lost."

Like automatons they turned to see where the voice had come from, and found Piero and François advancing on them.

They pulled apart with jerky movements.

"You should be more careful, Vanda," Robert said, speaking roughly.

"Yes," she said, scarcely knowing what she said. "Yes, of course."

It seemed to her that he turned away from her abruptly, striding off along the platform and leaving her with her two cavaliers.

She remained with them for the rest of the visit. Sometimes she would see Robert in the distance, deep in conversation with an official of the Tower, apparently discussing some technical point. It must have been absorbing, because never once did he glance up at her.

Piero and François put themselves out to entertain her, making sallies, joking with each other and laughing immoderately when she ventured to make a witticism.

At last she became annoyed by Robert's refusal to meet her eye. Plainly he regretted the moment of silent, intense communication and was warning her that it meant nothing.

Very well. It meant nothing to her either and she would make that plain to him.

Nothing could have been merrier than the way she flirted with both young men, teasing them one by one, then together, with the supreme assurance of a woman who realised her own power.

And nothing could have been more indifferent than Robert's behaviour. He descended from the Tower with a handful of leaflets to sit in the carriage, absorbed in reading them and apparently oblivious to everything around him. As they drew up outside the hotel, François was saying,

"Then it is all settled."

"What is settled?" Robert enquired.

"We are going to the opera tonight," Vanda told him.

"My parents rent a box which we may use," François explained. "We will call for you at seven o'clock."

He kissed Vanda's right hand. Piero kissed her left hand.

"I am surprised you have any hands left, the way they devour them," Robert grumbled as they walked upstairs.

"Oh, don't be so disagreeable," she retorted. "I find their attentions charming."

She was pleased to find that the dress shop had delivered several items while she was away. She and her maid spent the next hour in delightful conference as to what she should wear for the evening.

She finally decided on ivory silk, draped in the front in a manner that managed to be both modest and immodest. The neckline was of a respectable height, yet the drapery drew attention to her magnificent bosom.

She completed her attire with long, dancing pearl earrings, such as could only be worn by a woman with a swan-like neck. More pearls adorned her neck and wrists and a pearl tiara crowned her hair. They were all perfectly matched, and actually more valuable than her diamonds.

When Robert came to collect her, she had to admit to herself that he looked very smart in his formal white tie and tails.

How handsome he was! But it was not just his looks, she realised, which drew her eyes. There was an extra 'something' about him, which made him different from all the other men.

She could not precisely define it, but she knew it would make every woman look at him in admiration.

But why should she care? She had plenty of admirers of her own.

Robert nodded when he saw her.

"Excellent," he said. "The Paris Opera is a place of splendour and you will be able to make a grand entrance."

"Thank you, kind sir," she said, concealing her disappointment behind an ironic manner. Surely he could have said something a little more personal?

"Do you know," she said, "I actually forgot to ask which opera it is."

"Does it matter? You are going to be seen, not to see. Your pearls alone proclaim that."

"Oh, these," she said airily.

"Yes, those. The famous Sudbury pearls, worth a king's ransom. You should receive at least three proposals on the strength of them."

"If you are daring to suggest that I would be so vulgar as to – "

"Spare me your indignation. Your suitors may be impressed. I am not. Here's your fan, here's your purse. It is time we were going."

It was exactly the speech a brother might have made. Vanda had no choice but to take his arm and depart, seething.

But her annoyance faded as they descended the stairs together. She knew they made a fine looking couple.

To her surprise there were three people waiting. The Countess had decided to join them. She greeted Vanda charmingly, while her eyes flickered over the pearls. For Robert she produced a ravishing smile.

"You don't mind if I squeeze into the box with you?" she cooed.

It turned out that 'squeeze' was exactly the right word. With five of them the box was a tight fit, so that the Countess needed to sit very close to Robert, which seemed to trouble her not at all.

Vanda refused to look at them. If he wanted to make

a fool of himself by flirting with a married woman, that was no business of hers.

The opera was *Manon*, by Massenet, the story of a woman of pleasure who fell in love but ultimately paid the price for her sins.

In the interval the Countess was full of sentimental yearning.

"How tragic," she sighed. "But for all its sadness *Manon* is a great love story, don't you think?"

She turned melting eyes on Robert.

Vanda allowed herself to be drawn out into the corridor by her two cavaliers.

She told herself that she was having a wonderful time, a time of champagne and romance. But somehow her heart was no longer in it. And her thoughts were directed behind the closed door of the box, where Robert and the Countess were alone together.

"Shall we return?" she said at last. "I am sure it's very impolite for us to leave them alone for so long."

The lights were just dimming as they entered the box, so Vanda could not be quite sure whether Robert and the Countess had really been gazing into each other's eyes. She sat determinedly concentrating on the stage until the next interval.

When the lights came on again, Robert rose to his feet and declared his intention of seeking the bar. The whole party left the box together and before long the Countess drifted away to talk to friends who had hailed her.

François drew Vanda's hand through his arm and led her aside for a private talk, leaving Robert no refuge from Piero, who was determined to speak to him.

"I am glad of this chance of a moment alone with you," Piero said. "There are many urgent matters I must say to you."

"Really?" Robert replied in a cool tone that would have warned a more perceptive man. "I am surprised that you can spare the time from saying 'urgent matters' to Va – to my sister."

"Ah, you have noticed? *Bene!* I am glad, because it is about her that I must say urgent things to you. Never did I think to meet such a woman. It is incredible that she is still unmarried."

"She is a widow."

*"Si,* she has been telling me all about her beloved husband and their great tragedy. She says her heart is dead and I must ask you if you believe that is true."

"If her heart is – how the devil should I know?" Robert demanded, wild-eyed.

"But you must know her better than anyone."

"I thought I did," Robert muttered.

"Pardon?"

"Nothing. Yes, I suppose I know her reasonably well."

After this there was a pause, during which Piero meditated on English coldness and Robert wondered how soon he could bring this interview to an end.

At last Piero resumed,

"Then you can, perhaps, tell me if it is too soon for her to love again?"

"If it – ? What does she say?"

"Alas, she says nothing. She only laughs to hide her broken heart. But you are like a Papa to her, *si?"*

"No," the Earl answered firmly.

Piero looked puzzled.

"But you are the head of the house. You have authority. It is unthinkable that she would marry without your consent."

"My sister is not known for recognising any man's authority. Her husband had endless trouble with her, so be warned."

But Piero had evaluated the pearls and would not be warned.

"Such a spirited lady," he sighed.

"That is as may be," Robert said tersely, "but you should be aware that I consider it my duty to guard my sister from entanglements. Now I believe it is time for us to return to the performance."

The last act was a trial to everyone and each of them, for their own reasons, was relieved when the curtain finally came down and they were free to leave.

The Countess was persistent in begging them to join her for supper. Robert and Vanda were equally resolute in refusing, leaving her with no choice but to drive them back to their hotel in her carriage, bid them goodnight, and drive away.

"I think I shall order a large pot of tea," Vanda suggested. "Will you join me?"

"Gladly. Plain English tea will be a relief after the wild Latin passions of the evening."

"Yes, the music was very emotional, wasn't it?"

"I wasn't referring to the music," he said grimly.

He joined her in her room half an hour later and they drank the first cup of tea in silence.

"I thought you would have wanted to join the Countess for supper," Vanda said. "The three of us could have made ourselves scarce."

"Thank you for that kind offer," he said wryly. "I am glad you didn't."

"But why?" Vanda asked. "Surely you enjoyed her company this evening?"

"To a certain extent," Robert replied. "But she is a little too determined to overwhelm me."

"Yes, I noticed that. What would her husband say?"

"Nothing. I imagine he's glad. She has given him three sons and a daughter, so if she now chooses to lead her own life, it leaves him free to lead his."

Vanda was silent for a moment. Then she remarked,

"Of course that is nothing new. There are couples who live that way in London. I have met them, and I am sure that you have. As long as they are discreet, Society thinks nothing of it. But it would not suit me."

"Nor me. When I marry I shall expect my wife to be as faithful to me as I shall be to her."

"You say that now," Vanda said with a slightly teasing note. "But when your nursery is full, both you and she might be glad to follow their example and lead separate lives."

"Never," he said fervently.

Vanda chuckled. "So you did not enjoy the Countess's 'wild Latin passions'. I wish I knew what she said to you."

"You never will," he replied coldly. "And I was not just referring to her. Piero was asking me all sorts of questions about you. If I am not mistaken he plans a proposal and wanted to know if I would agree."

Vanda gave a small choke that ended in a giggle.

"Yes?" he asked in a dangerous voice.

"Did you give your consent?" she asked in a muffled voice.

"I left the matter open. There was very little else I could do since I didn't know exactly what stories you had been telling him. He cannot keep his eyes off your pearls, but I have a feeling it is more than that. Was your late husband a millionaire by any chance?"

Vanda made a vague gesture.

"I may have gilded the lily a little bit."

"A little bit? Enough to make him want to marry you. I have always warned you that your tongue would get you into trouble."

"But it is so easy. You just have to refuse him on my behalf."

"Oh, no," he said hastily. "I want no part in this. You can tell him yourself. That will teach you to be more careful next time."

"I cannot believe that my dear brother would decline to protect me," she said with a melancholy sigh.

"Any more of your games, miss, and your 'dear brother' will decline to have anything further to do with you. And don't laugh. It isn't funny."

"It is," she said. "It is terribly funny. I wish I could have seen your face when Piero was talking to you."

He grinned.

"He wanted to know if it was true that your heart was dead after your great tragedy."

"Robert, he never said that!"

"He did, I swear it. I don't know how I kept a straight face. Then he said he was sure you would never marry without my consent, as I stood in the position of your father."

Vanda burst out laughing and Robert joined in.

"I told him he was mistaken," he said in a shaking voice. "I am not in the least like your father."

"No, you are not," she responded firmly.

And suddenly the laughter stopped and a nervous silence fell between them. For he was definitely not her father.

"Goodnight," he said, rising hurriedly and leaving the room.

63

# CHAPTER FIVE

For the Fontellac Ball, Vanda chose diamonds, because they looked so well with the black velvet gown she was wearing.

"You will be the attraction for all eyes," Robert told her. "A woman of mystery, romance and great wealth. That is the idea, isn't it?"

"You can make fun of me if you like," she huffed. "I don't care."

"When I think of what your scheming could involve me in, I have no desire to laugh," he told her darkly.

He was dressed as he had been the night before and looked so handsome that Vanda told herself it was positively unfair.

A carriage took them to the Fontellac estate which lay just outside Paris. From a distance the Chateau came into view, blazing with lights in the dusk. Strains of music reached them faintly.

Carriage after carriage was entering the huge wrought iron gates and proceeding up the long drive.

As they drew up outside the entrance a powdered footman stepped forward and let down the carriage steps. Robert handed Vanda down, and together they walked to where the lights beckoned them.

The Countess greeted Vanda with a kiss, while her

eyes flickered over her, checking her jewels. Then all her attention was for Robert and the luxurious smile she gave him made it only too clear that she regarded him as a potential lover.

As Vanda entered the ballroom a footman handed her a dance card, in which she would enter the names of her partners. Piero and François immediately scribbled their names in it and would have taken every dance if Robert had not intervened.

"No more than two dances with the same gentleman, sister dear," he said smoothly. "Give the others a chance."

"You are right," she agreed. "It will make for more variety."

"But you must start the evening with champagne," François said, positioning himself on one side of her.

"That's what I was going to say," Piero protested, stationing himself on the other side.

"Well I said it first!"

"Hush," Vanda reproved them. "You can both supply me with champagne."

They applauded this idea and the two of them went off together.

After that she was never short of admiring company. Gentlemen crowded around her, paying her compliments, exclaiming over her beauty. Only a few were vulgar enough to glance too obviously at her magnificent jewels.

The whole evening seemed to spin around her in a haze of magical blur. She had never enjoyed a ball so much. The only disappointment was that Robert did not ask her to dance with him.

Of course, that might be difficult, since he was officially her brother, she reasoned. But she could not prevent her eyes lingering on him, as he whirled by with some beauty in his arms.

Too often that beauty was the Countess.

'Only two dances indeed!' she thought crossly. 'I am sure that must be their third.'

Their hostess was resplendent with feathers in her hair and a vast array of jewels. There were so many of them it was difficult to see her beneath them.

Vanda was not really surprised when she overheard a lady commenting to a gentleman,

"Our hostess glitters like a Christmas tree. I wonder who paid for all those costly baubles she is wearing."

"I doubt if you could count a list as long as that," came the sarcastic answer.

The lady laughed.

"I have always heard that she expects her lovers to pay up in one way or another. The jewels she wears now are to impress us with how many lovers she has had, and is still having."

There was no doubt from her scathing tone that she was jealous. She was regarding her companion possessively, as though afraid that he might be the next on the Countess's list.

But he did not see her look. His eyes were on the Countess.

Vanda lost track of her own partners. They all gazed at her with hot eyes. Some tried to hold her improperly close and one of them murmured,

"You are adorable. It intoxicates me to be so close to you. Why don't we slip away upstairs, so that I can show you how much closer I want to get?"

After a moment's shock, Vanda remembered how she had seen couples leaving the ballroom together and not returning.

With a sudden frisson of alarm she twisted her head

until she could see Robert. To her relief he and the Countess were still dancing in plain sight.

"Let us go," urged her partner, trying to ease her towards one of the doors.

Vanda realised that she was supposed to be a widow, and therefore an experienced woman of the world, adept at these situations.

But she was not going to allow herself to be spoken to like this. A moment later the man gave a yelp of anguish as a sharp heel dug into his foot.

"I am so sorry," she said sweetly. "I cannot think how I came to be so clumsy."

He gave her a fractured smile and limped painfully away.

The dance had not finished, so now she could enjoy a few moments to herself. It was a good chance to escape.

Nearby she spotted a pair of French windows standing open and hurried through them into the garden. It was wonderful to be courted and admired by so many men, but for the moment she needed a rest from them all.

The grounds were full of enchantment. Lamps hung from the trees, half illuminating shady paths that vanished into darkness.

It was a night for love, but only if the right man had been with her.

*"Signora!"*

Vanda winced at the sound of Piero's voice. Definitely he was not the right man. She had enjoyed flirting with him, but his endless compliments and declarations were beginning to pall.

A compliment from a man who never normally paid them, now *that* would be thrilling. Unfortunately there seemed little chance of it happening.

*"Signora,"* Piero cried again.

Vanda turned and smiled at him, spreading her fan and holding it in front of her like a shield.

"Ah, you run away to tease me," he breathed.

"No, I came here for some fresh air."

"The moon is beautiful, *si?* But not as beautiful as you. It is a night for love, *la bella notte* when we can be true to our hearts – what did you say?"

"Nothing," she said hastily.

In fact she had muttered, "Heavens, not again!"

To make up for her rudeness, Vanda gave him a charming smile. It was a mistake.

"How it warms my heart when you smile at me," he declared.

"Piero – "

"No, I must speak. Too long I have kept silent. Since the moment I met you I have loved you. I am mad with love, on fire with love, I dream of you all the time – "

He continued in this vein for some time, while Vanda tried not to laugh. Far from inspiring her romantically, Piero now seemed merely foolish.

"I wish you would not talk like that," she said.

"But how else am I to prove my devotion?"

"You do not need to. I believe you."

"Then you will marry me?"

"I did not say that."

"But you cannot refuse me," he cried passionately.

"Yes I can," she retorted in her most brisk and businesslike voice. "And I do."

*"Ah, mio Dio! Voglio morire."*

This time she did laugh.

"Nonsense, of course you don't want to die. Please Piero, no more of this nonsense."

"You can never love me. I am desolate."

"Stop being such a silly boy."

His answer to that was to seize her and plant a kiss on her lips. She ducked but his mouth just managed to touch hers before she could avoid it.

She was about to slap his face, not hard but just enough to make him see reason, when they were both stunned by the sound of a wail from the darkness of the trees.

The next moment François staggered out into the soft light.

"Traitor!" he screamed at Piero. "Betrayer!

He appealed to Vanda.

"Do not believe him. It is I who love you. Tell him that you belong to me."

"I do not belong to either of you," Vanda asserted, beginning to lose her temper. "Do stop acting like a pair of clowns."

Piero turned reproachful eyes on her.

"I do not understand you," he wailed pathetically. "I only know that I love you."

"And *I* love you," François declared.

He tried to seize her hand, but she snatched it away. In the same moment Piero also attempted to take hold of her.

Without hesitation Vanda brought down her fan first on Piero's head, then on François.

"Perhaps you will understand that!" she exclaimed. "I have no patience with either of you."

"Do not judge me by this imbecile," François begged, rubbing his head.

"Ignore him," Piero gasped, also rubbing. "You were mine first, and you always will be."

"I am nobody's and you are making fools of yourselves," Vanda said. "Now, that's enough."

Determined to hear no more, she turned and almost ran across the lawn back to the house. At the French windows she looked back, to see if they had dared to pursue her.

On the contrary, they had so far forgotten her as to become absorbed in their hostilities. She could just about see them squaring up to each other under the trees, and hear the odd shouted word.

'So much for undying devotion,' she thought wryly.

She slipped back into the ballroom just as the music was finishing. She looked round and was glad to discern the Countess talking to somebody. So she and Robert had not 'slipped away upstairs.'

Not yet, anyway, she thought darkly.

And then suddenly Robert was at her elbow.

"Can you spare a dance for me, sister?"

"Well, my card is really rather full," she said, opening her dance card and pretending to consider. "But perhaps I could find you one later – "

"To blazes with that," he said, whisking it out of her fingers and tossing it away. "The others will have to wait. I am exercising my rights as your male guardian."

"You are no such thing," Vanda replied. But her protest was mechanical. She was far more occupied by the feel of his arm encircling her waist as he swept her into the waltz.

It was exhilarating to be held so firmly, yet so lightly. She could dance like this forever. How strange that she had never felt this sense of excitement when they had danced together in the past.

But somehow those days felt like a different world. Something strange and new was happening, something that she did not understand, but which made her feel that she was on the brink of momentous discoveries.

She looked into Robert's face, trying to discover any trace of the feelings that were beginning to possess her. But she saw only the humorous irony that was his normal look.

That calmed her and put her on her guard. Not for the world would she allow him to suspect what was happening to her.

What *might* be happening to her, she corrected herself. It would be very foolish to allow herself to fall in love with him and she could only be glad that she had detected the danger in time.

"At any rate," he said, "I am a very poor guardian to allow you to disappear into the garden alone with Piero."

"Then why did you?" she asked impishly.

"I was prevented from coming after you by the Countess, hanging on my sleeve and making foolish chatter. By the time I had dislodged her it was too late. Did you behave yourself out there?"

"Perfectly."

"I enquire because I was a little surprised to see you return alone. Has Piero shot himself for love?"

"How can I tell?" she replied lightly. "He was certainly alive when I left."

"Heartless minx! I have been watching him throughout the evening and he has definitely been suffering. He thought he would keep you to himself, but you were surrounded by courtiers at every turn."

"It has all been very enjoyable."

"Has anyone knelt at your feet and begged you to love him?"

"Two men tried to kiss me after I had danced with them. But I told them that my brother guarded my honour very severely and would shoot any man who tried to make love to me!"

"Did they believe you?" he asked.

"Oh, yes. I explained that you had already shot two men through the heart."

"You told them *what?*"

"Well, I had to say something. They were getting out of hand."

"And the gentleman you sent off the floor limping?"

"Ah, that's a long story."

"You mean it's a shocking story?"

"Let's just say that I will tell you another time. In the end I sought some peace in the garden."

"Closely followed by Piero. And François. Or did you not see him?"

"I believe he was there," she answered vaguely. "I may have caught a glimpse of him."

Robert looked at her cynically, but said no more.

As the music slowed he began to say,

"I think you should stay by me for a while, in case you set the place into an uproar – "

He was interrupted by a cry from the garden and a flustered young man rushed in.

"A duel!" he cried. "Piero and François. A duel."

"Oh, no!" Vanda gasped. "Surely they cannot really be fighting a duel. Robert, we must stop them before they hurt themselves."

"Calm yourself. I shall be very surprised if this does not turn out to be another piece of foolery, which is about all those two are capable of. Really Vanda, whatever did you do to provoke this drama?"

"Why do you assume that it's my fault?" she demanded indignantly.

"Because I am beginning to know you."

"You have known me for years."

"I thought so too, only to find myself quite mistaken. Come along, let's go and witness this farce."

She was rather indignant at such a way of dismissing the subject. While she did not want anyone to be hurt, she was not really averse to two handsome young men duelling over her charms.

Everyone in the ballroom streamed out into the grounds, eager to witness the diversion, but nobody could really take the duel seriously.

And they were right. Piero and François were under the coloured lamps, squaring up to each other in the kind of fancy dress that could only have come from a child's nursery.

Each had slung a cloak over his shoulders. The cloaks were designed for children, but still managed to swirl flamboyantly.

Each wore a paper hat on his head and they wielded swords that looked impressive but were blunt and made of wood.

As soon as Vanda made her appearance they ran to her, each taking a hand and drew her forward to stand on a small incline in the ground. Standing there she was like a queen, looking down on the proceedings.

Then, moving in perfect unison, they stepped back and raised their wooden swords to her.

"We who are about to die salute you," François cried melodramatically.

They turned to confront each other.

*"En garde!"* they cried.

Two wooden swords clashed. For the next few minutes they strove back and forth with grim determination while the crowd cheered, laughed and clapped.

At last Piero took a mighty swipe at his opponent, knocking his sword from his hand with a force that broke it and sending him staggering back until he fell full length on the grass.

The spectators roared with delight. Robert too grinned at the comedy, until he saw Piero stride purposefully towards Vanda.

"I am the victor and you are mine," he proclaimed.

He would have taken hold of her, but Robert reacted quickly. With a mutter of, "Oh, no, you don't!" he sprang up the incline, seized Vanda up in his arms and made a run for it.

"Hey!" she cried as she felt herself being swept along willy-nilly. "What do you think you are doing?"

"Putting an end to this nonsense once and for all," he stated firmly.

"But you have no right. Put me down."

"No, and that is final."

To emphasise his point he tightened his arms around her. Vanda felt the pressure and suddenly her head swam. She looked up at his face with a hint of eagerness, but she could see only exasperation and grim determination.

The next moment she felt herself being tossed into a carriage like a bag of flour. Robert climbed in after her and they were away.

"From now on," he said, "you are going about with a sack over your head!"

"That won't help," she screamed, struggling up into a sitting position and joining battle. "I am a great beauty, remember? I can shine through any sack."

*"Two* sacks. Understand me, from now on you are going to behave yourself with complete decorum."

"Am I? Are you sure of that?"

"Quite sure," he asserted repressively.

"We will see."

"Vanda, I am warning you – "

She gave a provocative little chuckle, beginning to enjoy herself again. There was something to be said for bickering with Robert. She could count on his full attention.

They continued the argument all the way back to the hotel, but he was no longer annoyed and nor was she. He leaned back in his corner of the carriage and regarded her with cynical appraisal, until he noticed something that made him concerned.

"You are shivering," he remarked.

"Well you made me leave without my cloak," she protested, running her hands over her bare arms and shoulders.

"My poor girl. That was indeed thoughtless of me. Yes, it's turning cool in this night air."

"I shall probably contract pneumonia," she sighed pathetically. "And it will be all your fault."

He grinned.

"Stop trying to make me feel guilty, you little witch. Here, take my jacket to keep you warm."

He stripped it off and wrapped it gently around her shoulders. Vanda shivered pleasurably and snuggled down inside its protection.

"Thank you," she said with a meekness that made him regard her with renewed suspicion.

Her eyes met his, bland and innocent.

His grin turned into a smile of real warmth, which she met with one of her own. He slipped his arm around her shoulders, drawing his jacket even closer about her, and they finished the journey in harmony.

When they reached her door he said,

"Perhaps it is time we thought about leaving."

"So soon?"

"Haven't you brought enough men to your feet? Wouldn't you like to explore pastures new, and slay some more victims?"

"I have not finished with Paris yet," she retorted in a teasing voice.

"Come, the whole of Europe lies before us. Think of the conquests you can make."

"That's very true," she said, regarding him mischievously. "But are you sure that you can stand the strain."

He groaned.

"No, I am not. I will swear on my life that living with my five real sisters has not prepared me for you. I had no idea that being a brother could be so exhausting. What else will you teach me before our trip is through, I wonder?"

"Perhaps it is you who will teach me?" she mused.

"I cannot believe there is anything I can teach you," he asserted wryly. "You seem mistress of every situation."

"You forget how long I have been mistress of my father's house."

"That's not what I – " he checked himself with an awkward laugh. "No matter. I bid you goodnight."

"Goodnight," she said and entered her own room with a smile.

Half an hour later, when she had finished undressing and was sitting whilst her maid brushed her hair, she heard a knock on her door. When the maid opened it, she found one of the hotel servants with the cloak that Vanda had left behind at the Chateau.

"It was delivered downstairs by a young gentleman who would not leave his name," she reported.

In the next room Robert heard the door open followed by a murmur of voices. But by the time he had put on his dressing gown and looked out into the hall there was nobody to be seen. Frowning, he shut his door and retired to bed.

He was just sinking contentedly into sleep when the night was rent by a strange sound from below.

*"Bella signora – la mia bellissima – "*

Someone was singing in a light tenor voice that floated up through the night. The sound was not entirely displeasing, but it was not what a tired man wanted to hear at this hour of the night.

Groaning, Robert rose, walked to the window and threw it open, looking down onto the hotel garden.

There, just as he had feared, was Piero, standing on the grass directly beneath Vanda's window, arms raised and head thrown back as he carolled up to her.

*"Amore – amore – "*

"What the devil do you think you're doing?" Robert called down to him.

"I am proclaiming my love to the world," Piero declared joyously.

"Making a devil of a racket, you mean! For pity's sake, be silent."

"My love can never be silenced," Piero shouted. "It cries to the heavens!"

"Well it had better not," Robert snapped. "How dare you make an exhibition of my sister!"

"She will forgive me – "

"Not if I have anything to do with it."

To the right of him he heard the sound of a window being opened and Vanda appeared on her balcony, dressed in a becoming robe of peach satin. Her black hair hung down to her waist in a fashion he had never seen before.

*"Amore,"* Piero cried, "how beautiful you are with your hair loose and flowing. In just the way I have seen in my dreams."

"The devil you have," Robert snarled.

"Did you see that I returned your cloak?" Piero asked.

"Yes, I did, thank you."

"How could your so cruel brother be so barbaric, so indifferent to your comfort?"

"I often wonder that myself," she sighed.

"Vanda," Robert called urgently, "Go back inside."

"Why?"

"Because this is a most unsuitable scene for you."

"But it is about *me*. And your barbaric indifference, of course."

Robert ground his teeth.

"It is not appropriate for you to be involved," he demanded. "Kindly retire at once."

"But that would be most unkind when Piero has taken so much trouble."

To Robert's horror it now became apparent that the Italian was not alone. Three more figures emerged from the shadows and took up their positions on the grass. There was the plink of strings, the sounds of a flute, and an accordion.

"Oh, no!" Robert groaned.

To his annoyance he could see that Vanda was leaning over her balcony rail showing every sign of enjoyment at the spectacle.

Piero dropped down on one knee and began singing again.

*"La bella mia piccina –"*

"Vanda!" Robert called.

"Hush," she told him. "I am trying to listen."

"Do you know how unseemly this is?"

"What does it matter?"

*"Amore del mia cuore – "*

"What's that he says?"

"He says I am the beloved of his heart.    Isn't it romantic?"

"It's a load of dashed nonsense!"

"Stop being a killjoy!"

"Vanda, I am trying to get some sleep."

"Well, go inside and shut your window.    He isn't singing to you."

She gave the singer a little teasing wave, which Robert regarded with exasperation.  Had she *no* sense of propriety?

*"Cuore del mio cuore – "* Piero warbled.

The Earl scowled, thinking it was time for action before this idiot had them thrown out of the hotel. He turned away and disappeared inside.

Outside, Piero was just getting into his stride.    His voice soared with triumph as he saw Robert, apparently in retreat.  Emboldened, he reached for a very high note and hit it successfully.

But that was his last moment of glory.  The note was cut off in its prime, ending in spluttering, as though the singer had just been doused with a large quantity of water!

After that there was peace and silence.

# CHAPTER SIX

The next morning Vanda breakfasted alone in her room. After waiting for her in the restaurant downstairs, Robert came to find her.

He was forced to admit that she looked a picture sitting at a table in the alcove by the window. The sun, streaming into the room, brought out blue highlights in her black hair. Her gown was made of soft fine wool in a delicate tawny shade that suited her perfectly.

For a moment his admiration checked the words he had meant to utter. But the moment passed.

"You might have informed me of your decision to take breakfast in your room," he said.

"I saw no need to inform you," she declared in austere tones. "I did not wish for your company this morning."

"May I enquire why?"

"I should have thought that the reason must be perfectly obvious to you," she replied, in a voice that was even cooler. "Your behaviour last night was not that of a gentleman."

"My behaviour was that of any reasonable man driven beyond endurance by nauseating sentimentality."

Vanda regarded him as she might have done a worm.

"Is it nauseating for Piero to declare his love for me?"

"It is if he does it to the whole world. I would think more of his so-called love if he declared it in private."

"What you think is neither here nor there. Piero does not seek your approval, sir, and neither do I."

"For pity's sake, Vanda, stop talking like the heroine of a cheap melodrama. Piero is after your fortune."

Her magnificent eyes flashed.

"Indeed? That's your opinion of me is it? That no man could want me unless tempted by the promise of money? What an insult!"

"I did not say that," he said. "And stop trying to pick a quarrel with me. I am wise to your tricks these days."

"I don't know what you mean."

"Yes, you do. You do these things just for the pleasure of seeing men run around you. I thought you had more sense than that, Vanda."

"I used to. I have had 'more sense than that' all my life. Now I am discovering what fun it can be not to have sense.

"You are a man, Robert. Men always enjoy freedom, so you cannot understand how badly I want to be free. I want to feel that I can make up my own mind and do what suits me."

"And what suits you is what happened last night, is it? A lunatic caterwauling under your window."

"I was enjoying it until you intervened – trying to order me inside as though you were my father."

"Perhaps I spoke a little too strongly. I merely disliked seeing him make an exhibition of you."

But that was the wrong point to make. Vanda jumped up from her seat and rounded on him furiously.

"Then you are going to be disappointed, sir, because

from now on I plan to spend every moment with Piero. And if you dare to disapprove, so much the worse for you!"

Robert too rose to his feet.

"Then let me make it clear that there are antics that I shall not tolerate from you."

"What I do is none of your business."

"As long as you are posing as my sister, your decorum – or rather your lack of it – is very much my business. From now on I prefer you to have nothing to do with this man."

"And let me make myself clear," she flashed. "I and I alone will decide who my friends are. You have no authority over me."

"Vanda, we are leaving Paris today. I suggest you begin immediate preparations for our departure."

"I shall do no such thing. I am going downstairs now. I shall spend the day sightseeing. Perhaps Piero will accompany me."

Before he could reply she had placed her hat on her head and flounced out in high dudgeon.

Robert ground his teeth.

Had there ever been such an impossible, infuriating woman?

Had there ever been a woman so magnificent?

The memory of her dark, flashing eyes made him smile.

Then he thought of Piero and the way she revelled in the Italian's company, and his smile faded.

He guessed that he ought to have stopped her leaving. Always assuming that he *could* have stopped her. He was no longer sure of his power to prevent her from doing anything.

He headed for the door, wondering if he was in time to catch up with her.

But as he reached out for the handle, the door opened violently, Vanda came flying into the room and threw herself recklessly into his arms.

"Oh, Robert, it's really terrible!" she cried fiercely.

"Hey, steady there," Robert urged, holding onto her.

He stepped back into the room, kicking the door closed and keeping hold of her.

"What has happened to upset you?" he asked.

She was panting and wild-eyed.

"Something shocking," she howled, "something that throws all our plans into disarray."

He paled, but by now he was becoming accustomed to her taste for melodrama.

"Calm down," he said, "and try to tell me what has happened that is so dreadful."

"I was on my way downstairs when I saw him," she gasped. "Luckily I had time to step back and I don't think he saw me, but if he did, it is a crisis and I do not see how we are ever going to come out of it."

"Come out of what?" he asked, keeping his patience with an effort.

"It is just going to be *so* awful, and I don't know why we didn't think of something like this – "

"Something like what?"

"But what could we have done? I didn't know that he meant to come to Paris, and even if I had I couldn't – "

"Vanda, will you stop talking like a feather-brain and tell me what has happened? Who have you seen?"

She stared at Robert as if he were mad.

*"Him!"*

*"Who?* – before I strangle you!"

"Lord Cranbon – Papa's dearest friend."

"Good grief!"

"If he sees me – oh, he mustn't!  He simply mustn't."

"No, we have to leave here quickly," he agreed.

"But where shall we go?"

"To the railway station and then we will catch the first train out.  Going anywhere.  Start getting ready while I see to the bill.  Where was he when you saw him?"

"At the reception desk.  He seemed to be checking in."

"Let's hope he isn't still there."

"Does he know you?" Vanda asked anxiously.

"I am afraid he does.  Hurry now."

He slipped out of the room and along the corridor to the head of the stairs.  There he stopped.

Down below he could see Lord Cranbon, just as Vanda had described, still standing at the reception desk.  There was no chance of avoiding him.  Robert hastily returned to his room.

"John," he called to his valet.  "I need you to do something for me.  Go down to the desk and request them to send someone up here.  Say I am checking out but wish to avoid attention."

John departed.  Robert paced the room, wishing he could see how this scenario was all going to end.  It had seemed like an adventure when they had started, but now it contained the awkward possibility of scandal.

There was a knock at his door and he opened it to find Vanda.  She slipped inside quickly.

"I heard you return," she said anxiously.  "Is it all right?"

"Be patient.  I have had no time to do anything except send for someone to settle the bill here in privacy."

John had returned, bringing with him the manager of

the hotel himself, full of anxiety lest the Earl had found the hotel not to his liking.

"Not at all," Robert said in his most charming manner. "Both my sister and I have very much enjoyed our stay here, but our time is limited and we have far to travel."

"We want to see as much of Europe as possible," Vanda cried. "Vienna, Venice – "

"Ah, Vienna," the manager mused. "It is almost the most beautiful city in Europe, second only to Paris. And by leaving today you can catch the Orient Express."

"Oh, yes, let's do that!" Vanda exclaimed. "I have heard about it. It is supposed to be the most wonderful train in Europe, like a travelling luxury hotel."

"But does it travel today?" Robert asked. "Surely it only runs twice a week?"

"True, my Lord, but this is one of the days," the manager informed him. "I can send a messenger to the station to make reservations for you."

He bowed himself out, and Vanda made a little dance of excitement around the room.

"How wonderful!" she cried. "I do hope we can be gone soon."

"But you do realise," Robert said, beginning to be amused, "that you will be leaving Piero behind?"

"Who?"

Vanda's stare was a masterpiece of innocence.

"Piero," Robert repeated. "Surely you remember him – the man who worships the ground you walk on?"

"Oh, him."

*"Oh, him?* Is that all you can say about your devoted admirer?"

"Well, he was good fun for a while, but now I am ready for something different. It was beginning to become terribly tiresome with him making sheep's eyes at me all the time."

"You have recovered remarkably quickly from the admirer who made a romantic serenade beneath your window – "

"And who suffered a pitcher of water tossed over him," she reminded him tartly.

"It was the best method of dealing with yowling cats."

She giggled.

"Well, anyway, he is now in the past."

"Only an hour ago you were planning to spend the day with him."

"But that was just to annoy you," she said lightly. "I managed it, too."

Irrationally he began to feel indignant on Piero's behalf.

"Have you no feeling for the poor fellow?" he demanded. "After everything you said – "

"I don't remember what I said, or what he said. I only know that flirting with him was one of the jolliest interludes that ever happened to me. Now do let us hurry and be gone from here."

"You really are a heartless woman."

"I know. It's such fun!"

She hurried back to her own room before Robert's feelings could get the better of him.

Vanda could not remember when she had felt so happy. Piero's ardent wooing had filled her with delight, although not for one second had she mistaken his declarations as for real.

But what had delighted her even more had been the look she had occasionally surprised in Robert's eyes.

It had been a strange look, one she had never seen in him. If she had allowed her imagination to run riot she might almost think it was jealousy.

Robert, jealous of her?

Surely it was impossible.

She had never even thought of him in that way.

Except now and then, on summer nights, when she had gazed longingly at the moon, and allowed herself to dream –

But she had pushed those dreams away, remembering that he saw their relationship only as brother and sister and assuring herself that she saw it the same way.

Until now –

Then she pulled herself together. This was no time to be indulging in fantasies. She was the cool, calm, collected Miss Sudbury, known for her common sense and strength of character.

Besides, there was work to be done.

Together she and her maid plunged into the packing. Just as they had finished, there was a knock on her door. It was Robert.

"It's all settled," he said, coming in and closing the door. "We have reservations on the Orient Express, and I have settled the bill, so let's leave at once."

"How much do I owe you for my half of the bill?" she enquired.

"Can you wait until we have boarded the train?"

"As long as it is understood – "

"Vanda, for the love of Heaven! You may pay for the entire trip if you like. But first, please concentrate on what matters most and *move!*"

"All right, all right. There is no need to shout."

"There is every need to shout since you are the most obstinate, maddening – "

"I thought you said we needed to hurry," she reminded him sweetly.

"Yes," he concurred, resisting the temptation to tear his hair.

"Well then, let's hurry."

In a short time their luggage was loaded into a waiting carriage. They descended the great stairway cautiously, looking out for any sign of Lord Cranbon.

But luck was with them. He had already moved into his suite and they were free to run out into the sunshine, climb into the carriage and proceed on their way to the railway station, the Orient Express and Vienna.

Vanda exclaimed with delight when she saw the famous train. It had been running for six years and in that time it had set new standards of luxury for travel. The carriages that crossed Europe from Paris to the East were known as palaces on wheels with their plush upholstery, mosaic floors and mother-of-pearl marquetry.

She was escorted to her sleeping compartment, while Robert was shown to his own compartment next door. As she was looking around her in delight, Jenny, her maid, came in.

"Isn't it lovely, miss," she sighed. "And the seats will make such a comfortable bed when they are made up."

"Will you be comfortable, Jenny?"

"Oh, yes, thank you, miss. Second class here is like first class on any other train."

She pulled open a small pair of doors in the wall, revealing a tiny 'bathroom' with wash basin and taps. Next to it was a closet just big enough for a few clothes.

"I will unpack a few things that you'll need for tonight," she said, and started to work.

Vanda wandered out into the corridor and found

Robert, standing by a window and watching the preparations for departure.

"I will not be easy in my mind until we are moving," she said. "I keep expecting to see someone come running down the platform calling for us to stop."

At that moment the whistle blew.

"Here we go!" Robert said, smiling tenderly at her excitement. "Stop worrying."

He took her hand, squeezing it in reassurance. She squeezed back and they stood, laughing in delight as the train picked up speed out of the station.

A conductor appeared in the corridor beside them, saying,

"Dinner will be served in one hour."

"Is it really time for dinner?" Vanda asked, astonished. "Where has the day gone?"

"It has slipped away somehow," Robert agreed. "And we missed lunch. I will see you in an hour."

She chose the red velvet gown she had worn on the first night and Jenny dressed her hair elegantly. Her only adornment was a pair of tiny diamond ear-rings.

She knew she had made the right choice when Robert came to collect her at her door and she noticed a warm approval in his eyes.

"I have ordered champagne to be served as soon as we sit down," he said as he led her to the saloon.

As he had promised the waiter filled their glasses at once. Through the windows they could the red glow of the sun beginning to set. It glowed off the glasses as they raised them in salute.

"We are on our way," he said. "How your friends will miss you. I think of Piero, calling at the hotel, desolate to find you have fled – "

"Oh, forget Piero," she stated airily. "He will find another heiress in no time at all."

"Perhaps he was truly in love with you?" Robert teased.

"I don't think so. I am sure that true love doesn't sound so much like play-acting."

"And how does true love sound?"

Suddenly she felt self-conscious and could no longer look at him.

"I do not know," she admitted. "I have never heard it. Perhaps I never will. But I am sure it doesn't sound like Piero and François, full of bombast."

"How wise you have become. And don't say you will never find love. It is only a question of being patient."

"I have been patient a long time," she said with a wry little smile. "I am practically an old maid!"

"You seem to forget that I have been observing you these last few days. You have looked glorious, magnificent and splendid. But never like an old maid."

She laughed, blushing.

"Thank you," she said, surprised.

"And now tell me about all those gentlemen I saw whispering invitations into your ear last night."

"You don't know what they were whispering in my ear?"

"I think I do. I know the kind of words that can be whispered and I definitely saw one of them trying to guide you right out of the ballroom. Luckily for him he didn't succeed or I would have been forced to – er – what was it?"

"Shoot him through the heart," she reminded him.

"That's right. I knew I was supposed to do something dramatic! Was he saying what I thought?"

"He was inviting me to slip away upstairs so that we could 'grow close'."

"Serves you right for posing as a widow. He naturally assumed that you knew what he was talking about."

"I knew exactly what he was talking about. I just wasn't going to *do* what he was talking about. And now tell me about your adventures. I was sure you were going to 'slip away' with the Countess."

"She tried hard enough to make me," Robert admitted. "Nor was she the only one."

"Stop boasting."

"I am merely making the point that the ladies with the very highest titles are often the most free and easy in their behaviour. Some of the costliest jewels were adorning ladies with the souls of courtesans."

"Tell me more," Vanda said, wide-eyed.

"There was one woman in particular last night – I first met her when I was in Paris, some years ago.

"I had not inherited the title then and my father kept me on a strict allowance, so I felt fairly poverty stricken in that society. In fact I was just a looker-on.

"I was rather hurt as I thought myself devilishly attractive to the opposite sex. But I could not afford to decorate women with jewels, so they didn't waste their time on me."

Vanda smiled sympathetically. She realised it must have hurt him.

"So what happened when you saw her again last night? Did she recognise you?"

"How could she? The first time we met, I simply did not exist for her. But now I am an Earl with a fortune and she was all smiles – and – er – invitations."

"But you didn't accept her invitations?" Vanda asked.

Suddenly she was breathless because his answer was mysteriously important.

"No invitations from such a heartless lady could tempt me," he replied. "I have met too many of her kind."

He spoke lightly, but Vanda guessed that some trace of that old wound was still inside him and this was why he was so determined now to marry someone who loved him for himself.

He saw her looking at him and smiled a little too quickly. Then he changed the subject.

"We should start to plan our itinerary," he volunteered. "Are you very eager to see Vienna?"

A touch of constraint in his voice puzzled her.

"Would you rather not stay in Vienna?" she asked. "I have heard so much about what a romantic city it is, full of light and music."

"That was true once," Robert remarked heavily, "and one day perhaps it will be true again. But at the moment it is a city of darkness, full of tragedy."

Vanda's hands flew to her face.

"Tragedy?" she echoed. "Of course, I had completely forgotten."

Four months earlier Crown Prince Rudolf of Austria had committed suicide by shooting himself at his hunting lodge at Mayerling. Next to his body lay a beautiful young girl, Marie Vetsera, also shot.

"I have a friend in the British Embassy, and I hear a great deal," Robert told her. "Vienna is in mourning and the atmosphere is very tense because the authorities refuse to tell the truth about what happened. First they pretended that the Prince had died of poison.

"Eventually they were forced to admit that there was a bullet wound in his head. But they are still denying what everyone knows to be true, that it was a suicide pact."

"How terrible," Vanda whispered. Then she remembered something else.

"You met Prince Rudolf once, didn't you?"

"Yes, a couple of years ago, when he visited London for the Queen's Diamond Jubilee."

"And you liked him, I remember you saying so. You entertained him and the Prince of Wales one evening."

Robert grinned reminiscently.

"That's right. Buffalo Bill's travelling show had just arrived from America and we were all mad to see it. We drank too much and became very merry. But then the Prince grew morose and started talking about suicide, which he did frequently, according to one of his entourage."

Vanda was startled.

"As far back as that?"

"Yes. He was obsessed with the idea of ending his own life. But he seemed a good fellow, and I liked him a great deal then."

A faint stress on the word 'then' made Vanda look at him quickly.

"Not now?"

After a moment's hesitation he said,

"I once met Marie Vetsera as well. She was desperately trying to arrange an introduction to Rudolf. She idolised him from a distance as though he was an actor she had seen on the stage."

"Were you there when she finally met him?"

"No. It took her some time. She finally contrived to bring herself to his attention last autumn and a few months later she was dead."

"How horrible!" Vanda exclaimed.

"Exactly. The world is already beginning to call it a great love story, but I think what Rudolf did was despicable beyond belief. He was thirty with a wife and child and she was eighteen, little more than a child herself. That is not love, not as I understand it."

There was a new note in Robert's voice and it caused a stir in Vanda's breast.

"What do you understand by love, Robert?"

It was some time before he answered and when he did the strange note was present again.

"Giving," he said at last. "Putting the other person's needs first. If Rudolf had loved her he would have told her to stop being so silly, go home and find a way to be happy without him. Even if it had hurt him, true love would have made him do what was best for her."

He was silent again, and Vanda held her breath, not wanting to break the spell she could feel forming around them.

"I think," he continued slowly, "that if I loved a woman – I mean, really loved her – not just – "

"Not just an adventure," she prompted.

"Not just an adventure. I won't deny that I have had adventures. You have heard about some of them."

"Oh, yes," she said softly.

"But a woman you really love – that's different. At least, I think it would be. I have never felt that sort of love."

"Never?"

"Never," he repeated simply. "It sounds bad to say it, but in all my infatuations one part of my brain was alert for my own interests, always ready to pull out if she acted in a way that started warning bells ringing."

"What kind of way?"

"If she was too obviously interested in my fortune. I

might think she was wonderful, but suddenly I would look into her eyes and read the calculations."

"But you were calculating too," Vanda pointed out.

"Yes, I suppose I was. That is really my point. When I realised that part of me was standing aloof, it was the end."

"What was her name?" Vanda asked softly.

"What?"

"You are talking about one particular woman, aren't you?"

"Maybe I am. It's not important."

'*It is to me,*' she thought. But said nothing.

"One day I was infatuated with her," he added in a brooding tone. "The next day I had seen the danger and could not wait to escape.

"But if what I had felt for her had been real love, my defences would not have been bristling as they were. I would have cared more for her happiness than my own. I would have accepted any pain as long as she could have been happy, because that is what real love means."

"But can you ever find such a perfect woman?" Vanda asked.

He gave her a gentle smile.

"I did not say that she needed to be perfect, only that she had to possess that certain something that tugs at my heart. If she has that she can be as maddening as she likes, irrational, unreasonable – I can quarrel with her, laugh at her, or laugh with her. I may sometimes want to wring her neck, but that doesn't mean I do not love her."

He stopped. He seemed to have been talking in a dream. Now he looked like a man who had awoken to find himself in a new world.

"I am talking too much," he said abruptly.

"No, you are not," she smiled. "I like listening."

But he shook his head and adroitly turned the conversation into a different direction.

She longed for him to continue, but, wisely, she did not press him.

For the rest of the meal they talked lightly, but beneath the trivial words something was happening that was not trivial at all. It was momentous. Vanda could feel the air singing about her.

At last it was time to retire for the night. Robert escorted her to her compartment and remained watching her door until it closed.

Then he walked slowly to his own compartment, dismissed his valet and sat on the bed, staring at the far wall, seeing nothing but a woman's eyes, soft with tenderness or brilliant with laughter, gazing at him across a table.

Vanda found her bed made up and there was nothing to do but undress and slip between the sheets.

She lay in the darkness, intensely aware that Robert was just a few inches away on the other side of the wall. She felt strangely restless and sleep would not come.

She could not help listening and from time to time she could hear movement from beyond the wall, as though he too was restless.

After a long time she fell asleep.

# CHAPTER SEVEN

From Vienna they caught the ordinary train to Venice, which was nothing like the Orient Express. They arrived in the evening with just time to find a hotel.

For three days they wandered the beautiful city on the water, peaceful and happy, with no alarms or dramas. It was as if they had discovered a treasure that neither dared to touch, nor look at too closely, lest they find that it was not really there.

In the evenings they would find some tiny restaurant and sit over a glass of wine into the small hours, before strolling slowly back to the hotel. They said very little that could not have been overheard by the whole world. They seldom spoke of themselves or each other. And yet all the time the sensation of truth grew stronger, more urgent and more incredibly sweet.

On the fourth day they ran into an old Italian acquaintance of Robert's and their privacy was over.

"Now we must go and pay a visit to Duke Angelo and his family," Robert told her. "By this afternoon the grapevine will have told them that we are in Venice."

"Who is Duke Angelo?" she asked.

Robert rolled off a long, complicated name that she could barely follow.

"You are right," she remarked. "Duke Angelo is easier."

"He is a very important man in these parts. The Duchess was a great beauty and her son and daughters take after her."

The next day they hired a gondola to take them down the Grand Canal to the Palazzo Firese where the Duke and Duchess lived.

As he had predicted the grapevine had worked and as they approached the landing stage, the whole family came out to greet them.

"Elena," Robert said, "You are even lovelier than you were when I last saw you."

His hostess smiled at him and replied in English,

"You always pay the most delightful compliments. I have told my son he should emulate you if he wants people to think him charming."

Robert laughed.

Duke Angelo was a heavily built, middle aged man, who was still handsome. Vanda thought she might have been attracted to him once, but now she recognised that could never be possible.

He led them into the huge, ornate palace, with its elegant tiled floors and traditional decoration. Everywhere Vanda could see servants scurrying, arranging what seemed to be thousands of flowers in vases.

"Now our happiness is complete," the Duke sighed. "As you can see, we are celebrating and your arrival makes everything perfect."

"Our daughter is getting married tomorrow," the Duchess explained.

"Then we have picked the wrong time to intrude," Robert pointed out hastily. "Had we known – "

"Had you known, I hope you would still have visited us," the Duke said at once. "Of course you will attend the wedding. No arguments. It is settled."

As Robert had said, the young members of the family were as handsome as their parents. The most beautiful of all was the eldest daughter, Ginetta, who was to be the bride. She glowed with her love and when she spoke of her fiancé, Alberto, a look of special tenderness came into her eyes.

"We had to wait to be married," she confided to Vanda, because Alberto's father is only a Baron and Papa said I must not marry beneath me. But I told him that if my husband is a good man, then that is as high as a man can be, whatever his title.

"At first Papa was angry, but I told him that I would never marry anyone else. He and Mama introduced me to many suitors, but I refused them all, and after three years they gave in."

"Three years?" Vanda echoed, startled. "You waited for three years?"

*"Si,"* Ginetta said. "And for much of that time we were not allowed to see each other. But at last my parents realised that our love was strong enough to overcome any obstacle and so they agreed to our marriage."

She gave an impish chuckle. "Also they were afraid I would be an old maid. My sister Marcella wants to marry and that is not easy unless I marry first."

Vanda did not know what to say. She was awed by the powerful love and fidelity of these young Venetians. To wait for three years and not even be allowed to see the man she loved!

She wondered if she herself would be able to cope with such restrictions.

But she knew that it would be possible. If the man was the right one, the one to whom she had given her heart forever and was certain that she also possessed his, anything was possible.

But only the right man could give her the courage to

defy the world in lonely waiting.

She heard a sound from the garden and looked up. Robert was coming through the door, his form turned to a silhouette by the dazzling light outside against the muted light from within.

For a moment she could hardly see him and yet she knew it was him. She would have known him anywhere.

Only the right man –

"Is anything wrong?" he asked, walking towards her.

"Of course not," she responded, a little self-consciously.

"You looked strange, as though you had seen into another world."

"Perhaps I have."

"Are you going to tell me about it?"

Smiling, she shook her head.

"No, I do not think so."

"That is not like you. Normally you tell me what you are thinking."

"Well, as you said – *another world*."

She hurried away, leaving him looking after her with a slight puzzled frown and a question in his eyes.

As Ginetta had said, Marcella was also planning her marriage and her fiancé was present. He was a tall, aloof young man, with little conversation and Vanda found it hard to warm to him.

She felt much more at home with Alberto, a bright-eyed, eager young man, who could not take his eyes from his bride. The two of them seemed to be enclosed in an aura of love and joy.

The son of the house was Mario, handsome, nervous and as elegant as quicksilver. He was also extremely self-centred, although he covered it by huge charm. He sat next to Vanda over lunch and told her about his ambitions to be an artist.

"This afternoon I will take you to my studio," he announced, without asking if she liked the idea.

"Thank you," she replied, too amused to be offended.

As soon as lunch was over, he took her hand imperiously and whisked her away to the top of the great house. Here was his studio with windows in each of the four walls, so that light streamed in all the time.

"What a wonderful place!" she exclaimed, turning round and round in delight.

"Stay there!" Mario said suddenly, seizing up a sketch pad and making rapid strokes. "I want to catch you just as you are."

After a while he said,

"All right, now you can move. Look at me. Now move towards me slowly – slowly – that's right."

He was making more quick strokes. At last he showed her both pictures which he had created so quickly and she could see how talented he was. The full length picture was vivid with life and the face was indeed an incredible likeness.

"I shall keep these," he asserted, "so that I may study your beauty whenever I wish."

"Thank you, kind sir," she replied, politely, but not encouraging him.

"Is that how you accept a tribute to your beauty? Or have you received so many that you are now blasé?"

"I do not think any woman becomes blasé about compliments," she replied, "but she would be very silly to believe them all."

"But you must know how beautiful you are," he

continued insistently. "Just as you must know that I am at your feet."

"No, I did not know that," she responded lightly. "Nor do I really wish to know it."

"Ah, you are a mistress at luring a man on."

"I am no such thing."

"Any woman as beautiful as you knows the game that we are playing. Even to look at you inspires a man to want to draw you or perhaps to make love to you."

"I think he had better not try," she said firmly.

"But you are an inspiration to me. Naturally I want to kiss you and then I want – "

Now she was sure that she regretted coming up to his studio with this over-confident young man. Whoever she wanted to kiss, it certainly was not him.

"I think it is time for me to go," she said, turning to the door.

But before she could reach it, the door opened and Robert stood on the threshold.

"So there you are," he said to Vanda. "Ginetta told me you might have come to the studio with Piero."

"My name is Mario," said the artist.

"So it is."

"Then why do you call me Piero?"

"You remind me of someone I used to know," Robert said, giving him a deadly smile. "For the moment I cannot think who he is."

Vanda had to choke back the laughter. Her eyes met Robert's in a moment of perfectly shared amusement. And she found it every bit as sweet as the excitement that increasingly possessed her in his presence.

Ginetta and Alberto slipped into the room, holding hands.

"I was about to tell our guests about Greece," Mario declared, changing the subject diplomatically. "How it is a land of love and passion that inspires all artists."

"Oh, yes, I love to talk about Greece," Ginetta exclaimed. To Vanda she said, "that is where Alberto and I met."

"You met amongst the Gods of love," Mario proclaimed grandiloquently, "and they cast their benediction on you."

Ginetta giggled.

"Actually we met in the hotel lobby," she admitted.

"But the Gods of love are everywhere," Mario said. "So you still met beneath their kindly eyes."

"That is true," Ginetta agreed. "And then Alberto started to tell me all about the Greek Gods. Aphrodite and Eros, the Gods of love – and so many others."

"Look, I have painted them all," Mario shouted dramatically.

He began to pull out several canvases, all of brilliantly coloured figures representing the old Greek deities. There was Artemis, the huntress with her bow and arrow, Apollo, God of the sun, who also reigned over music, playing his lyre.

"That's Athene," he said, showing a woman with an owl on her shoulder. "Goddess of wisdom."

"There are so many Gods," Vanda breathed.

"Yes, there is a whole family of them in Greece," Mario said. "You choose one for every occasion."

"But the most significant ones are the Gods of love," Ginetta breathed.

She gazed adoringly into Alberto's face.

"They were the Gods who brought us together and gave us the courage to defy the world for our love."

"Yes, dearest," he breathed. "And they will keep us together and in love for always."

"That's why we are going back to Greece for our honeymoon," Ginetta announced. "We shall visit the shrines of the Gods, so that we can thank them for what they did for us. Then we shall marry again in an ancient Greek temple with the blessing of all the Gods."

"You talk about them as though they were real people," Robert observed, looking at them curiously.

"In a way they are real," Alberto agreed. "They have been our friends. They have protected us as they always protect true lovers. So we will start our marriage by going to see them and laying offerings of gratitude on their altars."

"But do not tell the Cardinal who will marry us tomorrow," Ginetta laughed. "I don't think he would quite approve!"

Vanda studied the pictures more closely, realising that Mario was almost as good an artist as he thought he was, because each of these figures was alive with personality.

Aphrodite's face was young and eager. Athene was calm and reflective. Hera, Goddess of marriage, was calm and a little smile played around her lips as though, after the hectic storms of passion, she had discovered the secret of true happiness.

"Ginetta is right," Robert mused. "They are somehow like real people."

"People that it would be so nice to meet," Vanda agreed with a little unconscious sigh.

Robert gave her a quick look, but said nothing.

They did not dine with the family that evening, but left them alone to finish preparing for the wedding.

As they strolled back to the hotel through the little alleys and across the bridges of Venice, Vanda paused beside a shop selling pictures and sculpture. The next moment she had darted inside.

"That figurine," she said when Robert followed her. "It's Aphrodite."

He looked closely at the marble piece which seemed that the wind was sweeping through its hair.

"It is very beautiful," he said. "But how can you be sure it's Aphrodite?"

"Oh, yes," said the shopkeeper. "She is Aphrodite, the Goddess of love."

"Then I should like to give it to Ginetta and Alberto," Vanda said. "As a wedding gift."

The shopkeeper named the price, which was considerable.

"Allow me to pay half," Robert offered.

"There's no need," Vanda protested. "I can afford it."

"I don't doubt it. But I should like it to be a gift from both of us – " he hesitated, "if that is what you would like, too."

He sounded unsure of himself. Vanda could never recall that happening.

"Yes," she said quietly. "That's what I would like, too."

They watched as the piece was wrapped up carefully.

"Is there a message to be enclosed?" the shopkeeper asked.

They chose a card and on it Vanda wrote,

*For those whom Aphrodite has blessed.*

She signed her name and Robert signed his beneath.

"Whom Aphrodite has blessed," he repeated, smiling at Vanda.

"It will be delivered to the Palazzo Firese within an

hour," the man said, writing a receipt for the money. "Good day to your Excellencies."

That night they dined in a quiet little canal-side restaurant, where the food and wine were both excellent.

"Why are you smiling?" Robert asked once.

"I was remembering how you talked to Mario, calling him 'Piero' and glaring at him. The poor man did not understand what was happening."

"On the contrary, he understood exactly what I meant to convey. He will never even think of kissing you again!"

"Were you listening at the door?"

"Certainly not."

"Then how did you know he wanted to kiss me?"

"My dear girl, give me credit for a little perception. I knew *that* while we were having lunch. I am only glad that I arrived in time to prevent him."

Vanda said nothing.

"Or didn't I?" he added slowly.

She gave him a gentle, provocative smile.

"You are the one who knows everything, Robert. Or do I give you credit for too much intelligence?"

"You will push me too far," he growled.

"Perhaps."

Apart from this exchange, they said very little. Each was deep in thought and each of them understood, without words, that they were thinking the same thoughts.

But neither was quite ready to talk about their feelings as yet. The force of what had swept over them had come as a shock, and the whole world seemed different.

"We should retire early," Robert said at last. "Tomorrow is going to be a long day."

As they left the restaurant, he drew her hand through

his arm and they meandered back to the hotel through the little streets in silent harmony.

*

For the wedding Vanda donned a summer gown of green silk organdie, embroidered with flowers and a stylish matching hat.

At ten o'clock a gondola called at the hotel, to convey them to St. Mark's Basilica, where the marriage service was to be held. In Venice it was traditional for a bride to travel to her wedding in a gondola and soon a huge convoy was gliding down the Grand Canal.

The sun poured down, glittering off the water, turning everything to light and joy. In a blaze of happiness Vanda turned to look at Robert to find him looking at her.

Soon they had reached the landing stage at St. Mark's Piazza. He assisted her out of the gondola and she felt the warm strength of his hands as he held her.

Alberto was already in his place, looking over his shoulder, although it was far too soon for the arrival of the bride.

All around her Vanda could see the huge church filling up with Italian aristocrats. This was a great Society wedding and everybody who was anybody had to be invited or they would feel insulted.

She supposed that if they had allowed her father to push them into marriage, it would have been the same, in a great cathedral in the presence of the highest Society.

But that is was not how Vanda would want it. If she married Robert she would need no grandiose setting, no huge choir nor aristocratic friends. She would require only a small country church, like the one on his estate, with their close friends to see them marry.

He would stand waiting for her, looking over his shoulder, just as Alberto. Perhaps he would be a little anxious in case, after all their squabbles, she changed her mind at the last moment.

But she would not change her mind. She would go to marry him with a heart full of glory. As she walked down the aisle, he would catch sight of her and his face would relax with relief. His eyes would shine with joy as she drew near. They would reach out to take each other's hands.

And he would make her his wife.

And then –

She drew a long breath.

Suddenly the organ burst into a triumphant peal. A ripple seemed to sweep over the congregation and Vanda awoke to the realisation that she had been lost in a dream.

A happy dream.

The happiest dream that she had ever dreamed.

Now Ginetta and her father were walking down the aisle. It was a long walk and it was only gradually that she came near enough for everyone to see how beautiful she was.

A dream bride, shimmering in white, a pearl tiara on her head, white roses in her hands and a long white lace veil flowing behind her.

But what Vanda saw most clearly was the look of blazing joy on Ginetta's face as she approached the man she adored, ready to be united with him forever.

The service began. Vanda could not follow the words, but she did not need words to understand the moment when the bride and groom exchanged rings. The looks they exchanged said, more clearly than anything else, that they had escaped the rest of the world and existed only for each other.

'That is how a bride and groom should look,' Vanda thought.

She glanced at Robert, but there was an expression on

his face that she could not read. She only realised that he too was transfixed by the sight of the bridal couple.

Soon the service was over and everybody was streaming out into the sunlight and across St. Mark's Piazza. Some hired gondolas for the journey to the palazzo. Others chose to walk the short distance.

Robert and Vanda strolled along slowly, both still in a daze from what they had witnessed. Bridges and canals floated past them in a golden haze.

They found the palazzo ablaze with life and rejoicing. The Duke greeted them with open arms.

"I should not have made them wait so long," he confided joyfully. "Any man who loves my daughter so much is the right man for her."

Then he could not resist adding,

"But it would have been nicer if he could boast a decent title."

The bride and groom were standing together, receiving their guests. As they approached, Ginetta seized Vanda's hands and kissed her on the cheek.

"Thank you both for our lovely wedding present," she sighed. "It is *so* exactly right for us."

In the next room they found the wedding gifts on display with Aphrodite in a prominent position.

"That is the best representation of Aphrodite that I have ever seen," said a kindly voice behind them. "A perfect Goddess of love."

They turned and found the Cardinal, smiling benignly.

"Of course, I have to pretend not to know," he said conspiratorially.

"Well, she *is* a pagan Goddess," Vanda said.

"And therefore I should disapprove?" he asked, his eyes twinkling with humour. "But I believe in anything that helps people to be true to each other. Love is so important, the most important thing in the world."

*The most important thing in the world.*

Vanda had heard such words in the past, but they had never struck her so forcibly as now. She thought about them all through the wedding feast, wondering why she had never understood this obvious truth before.

Then it was time for dancing. First the bride and groom danced alone together, her gown and veil swirling out in a white mist around her. They circled the floor once while the orchestra played a yearning romantic melody.

The Duke and Duchess also began to dance together, and all the other guests joined in.

Vanda was never without a partner. Mario, the Duke himself, the bridegroom, and a string of other men who made no impression on her. She danced with them all and forgot them.

Eventually the voice for which she had been unconsciously waiting said,

"Dance with me, Vanda."

Robert was there, holding out his arms and she moved into them gladly.

They had danced together before but this was different. Now they sensed something they had not known nor even suspected.

"You are beautiful, Vanda," he sighed. "More beautiful than any woman here."

She smiled.

"Are you making fun of me?"

"Why should you think so?"

"Because you have never paid me compliments before."

"Times change," he said seriously. "People change."

She could think of nothing but how it felt to be close to him. She wanted him to draw her even closer, to take her into his arms and kiss her.

Looking up, she met his eyes and was swept by an overwhelming conviction that he felt the same.

Suddenly his arms tightened about her and she felt herself being danced out of the tall windows into the garden.

Now, she thought happily, they could be alone and he could kiss her.

He swirled her around and around until they slowed and stopped beneath the trees. He moved his arms so that he could gather her into them, looking closely into her face.

"Vanda," he breathed softly. "Vanda – "

"Yes," she murmured.

She would have added, "my love," but a little uncertainty held her back. She wanted to hear him say it first.

"Vanda – "

There was a note in his voice that thrilled her. Her heart beat faster. He was drawing her closer, closer. At any moment his lips would touch hers.

But then she felt him grow tense and pull apart from her. A burst of laughter from somewhere in the garden had alerted them to the fact that they were not alone.

Vanda could have wept with disappointment. She wanted his kiss so badly,

"We should go in," he said unsteadily.

"Yes – yes, we must."

Reluctantly they walked across the lawn into the bright lights of the house, where everyone could see them and there was no further chance to be alone.

Vanda's mind was in turmoil. Now she longed to disappear from Venice, where everyone thought they were brother and sister and where they could not risk drawing closer.

If only there was some way of escaping now, this very minute.

The bride and groom were ready to leave. A boat was waiting for them at the landing stage, ready to carry them on the first stage of their journey to Greece.

A crowd gathered to wave them off. Ginetta tossed her bouquet into the air. It soared high and fell straight into Vanda's arms. A cheer went up.

Vanda buried her face into the white blooms to hide the fact that she was blushing. She had never felt so discomposed before. What would Robert think?

"And now," the Duchess was saying as they returned to the house, "we shall be free to give our friends all of our attention."

As she spoke she linked her arm with Robert's and gave him a significant look.

"But of course," the Duke added. "In fact, I insist that the two of you move into the palace and stay a long time with us."

Vanda held her breath. This was the last thing she wanted to happen, but could she be sure that Robert felt as she did? She waited, feeling as though her whole life was at stake.

And then, as though from a great distance, she heard him say wonderful, incredible words.

"You are too kind, my friends, but my sister and I cannot stay. Seeing Ginetta and Alberto has fired us with a desire to explore further. We shall leave immediately – to discover the secrets of ancient Greece."

# CHAPTER EIGHT

They departed from Venice the very next day.

"The manager of the hotel told me about a ship that cruises the Greek islands," Robert explained to Vanda. "There were two cabins left, so I secured them for us."

They were both delighted with the ship as soon as they walked aboard. It was luxurious with every modern comfort and it had been designed to reflect the atmosphere of Greece, even down to the names of the cabins.

"Believe it or not, my cabin is called Aphrodite!" Vanda told him as they leaned over the rail, watching the crew make ready to cast off from Venice.

"And mine is Apollo," said Robert.

The engines were humming and at last the ship began to move, gliding out into the open sea. Vanda stood at the rail, feeling the wind whipping past her, wondering what would happen in the mysterious future into which they were heading.

After the vibrant moment of last night, when she could sense him trembling with a feeling that seemed to reflect her own, Robert had returned to his normal manner, friendly but cool and ironic.

But surely everything would be different now? They were travelling to Greece, where they would find the Gods of love, as Ginetta and Alberto had discovered.

'Of course Greece is where we were meant to come from the very beginning,' she told herself.

But then she thought,

'Yet we needed to go to France and Italy first and make the discoveries that have ultimately brought us together.'

In her childhood she had read the stories of the Greek deities and been enthralled. But as the years passed and she grew up, she had forgotten most of them. Then, meeting the lovers in Venice and hearing them pay homage to the Gods who had united them, had brought all the tales back to her, as fresh and true as in the beginning.

"Are we doing the right thing?" Robert asked beside her.

"I am sure we are," she sighed eagerly. "I cannot wait to see the wonders of Greece."

"Perhaps the real wonders are the sights we cannot see," he ventured, "but which nonetheless are often the truest and purest."

Vanda nodded, feeling a great happiness at hearing him express a thought so much in tune with her own.

There was a restaurant on the deck and they enjoyed lunch in the sun, as the ship sped onwards.

"We are heading straight for the Gulf of Corinth," Robert explained, "without calling in anywhere else first. Tomorrow we will reach the Port of Itea, where we will stay for two days. From Itea we can travel the six miles to Delphi, the site of the oracle."

"I wonder if it will tell us the future," she mused.

He looked at her curiously.

"When you talk like that, it is almost as though you thought you were going to meet real people."

"Why not?" she asked. "Surely, with all the wonderful

114

events which have happened in Greece and the fact that the deities lived there for so long, they can still be found if one seeks them."

"I suppose you believe," he enquired, "that the Gods never die?"

"Of course I do," Vanda replied. "I have read so many books about them and found all the stories so fascinating. And then, seeing how Ginetta and Alberto have taken them into their lives and trusted their fate to them – how can I not believe?"

She looked so charming in her excitement that Robert could only smile.

The ship offered a small library full of books about Greece and they spent the rest of the day reading, preparing themselves for what to expect when they landed.

When she retired to bed, Vanda sat for a long time looking out of her cabin porthole at the moon shining on the dark sea, feeling at one with its mystery. It was late when she finally lay down to sleep.

The next afternoon they docked at Itea and hired a carriage which would take them to Delphi. Soon they were climbing the slope of Mount Parnassus, considered by the ancient Greeks to be the centre of the earth.

Here there was a sanctuary where the ancient Delphic priests performed a ritual, at the end of which the High Priestess, known as the Pythia, would answer the questions of those who consulted her.

Kings had come here and heeded her words, for they were considered to be the words of Apollo.

At last the carriage stopped and they stepped out into what had once been the most sacred temple of the ancient world. It stood in a huge natural amphitheatre, with steep inclines on three sides.

Vanda observed a raised stone circle, whose boundary

had once been surrounded by tall columns of which only three remained.

Two of them were joined by a lintel at the top, on which were carved two words in Greek. She knew, because she had read it in a book the day before, that the words meant, '*Know Thyself.*'

'And it's only since I have been travelling with Robert that I have come to know myself,' she pondered inwardly. 'How long have I loved him, and not understood?

'I understand everything now. I know that I love him, and that he is the only man I could ever love. If he does not love me in return, my life will mean nothing. Nothing at all.'

Exploring further, she found the entrance to the cave where the Pythia had received supplicants and dispensed her wisdom.

Vanda looked around to see if anyone was watching her. There were one or two other visitors wandering among the ruins and she could see Robert, kneeling down to study an inscription. But nobody was looking at her, and she slipped quietly into the cave.

At first there was a narrow passage, but then it opened suddenly into a wide space. Light came from two holes in the ceiling, pouring down in straight beams on the ruins of an altar below.

And suddenly the very air about her seemed to become alive and she felt a strong sensation that she was not alone. She looked around to see if anyone else had joined her, but nobody had.

And yet there was another presence. She knew that now with total certainty.

"*What do you ask?*"

The silence was unbroken, but the words were there, as clearly as if someone had uttered them.

"*Why are you confused?*"

"Am I confused?"

"*Only those who are in confusion and uncertainty seek my help.*"

"Can you tell me how this will all end?"

"*How do you wish it to end?*"

"I want him to love me."

After that there was a silence, stretching for so long that she was filled with dread.

"Tell me that he will love me," she begged.

"*I can promise nothing. Neither marriage nor happiness is certain. Even love is not certain. There are some who will never be loved, although they long for love all their lives.*"

"Am I one of them?" she asked in anguish.

"*You must have courage.*"

"Courage for what? To face the worst?"

Another silence, then at last the oracle's words whispered in her heart.

"*One will come speaking words that are sweet and false. Beware. Danger.*"

"What kind of danger?" Vanda asked. "Will this 'one' try to take him from me?"

"*I see trouble. That which was gained and lost will be sought again. I see danger. I see blood. I see death.*"

"Whose death?" she whispered.

Silence.

"Tell me more for pity's sake. Who will be in danger? Who will die? Not him, I beg you. Take me, not him."

But the silence continued. The Pythia had spoken, and had nothing more to say.

At last Vanda turned away. She had asked a question

and received an answer. Now she must wait to see what sense it made.

Slowly she left the sanctuary.

"There you are," Robert called, coming towards her. "I was looking for you."

"I came to consult the Pythia, to see if she had any words of wisdom for me."

He put his arm about her shoulders and squeezed them.

"What an odd creature you are."

"Why don't you ask too and see what she tells you?" Vanda suggested eagerly.

"No thank you. If something is going to happen, it will happen. Why spoil the surprise? Or then again, it might be something I would rather not know about."

'*I see danger – I see death.*'

"Robert please – just go down there once."

"It's getting late. The light is beginning to fade and we have to journey back."

He hugged her again. Looking up into his smiling face, she felt her worries begin to slip away. Why did she concern herself with superstition when he was here, so real and so warm?

"You have such a lot of common sense," she said, teasing him.

"I wish I could believe that that was a compliment."

"I never pay you compliments."

"True."

"Did the oracle tell you anything?" he asked.

"I am not sure. I did not understand."

"That is the way with oracles. Their prophecies can be taken in many ways, so they can always claim to be right."

"But it was so real – "

"Vanda, it was all in your head. Your own thoughts produced that prophecy – whatever it was. Nothing else."

Listening to Robert she felt her fears slipping away. She had imagined the Pythia's warning, because she was afraid to losing him. That was all.

"What did she say?" he asked.

"I cannot tell you. It is a secret."

He thought for a moment before questioning,

"Was it anything about us?"

Smiling, she shook her head.

"Tell me," he persisted.

"But I don't know. It was all so jumbled and confused, how can I tell if anything was about us? As you said, it was simply what I was telling myself in my head."

"But that is what I want to know most. What are you telling yourself about – everything?"

"I just cannot tell you," she repeated decidedly. "You might be telling yourself something different."

"I don't think so."

He tightened his arms and drew her close, not attempting to kiss her, but simply holding her against his chest.

Vanda nestled against him in deep peace and happiness, feeling his heart beat softly against her ear.

They were interrupted by a call from their driver, who was making gestures indicating that the light was fading fast.

"We should go," Robert said gently.

That evening they dined in the ship's main restaurant, which had been decorated to look like an ancient temple. But to Vanda it was all hollow and meaningless. She had been inside a real temple and she knew that it was nothing like this pale imitation.

"Are you all right?" Robert asked. "That cave didn't frighten you, did it?"

"No, of course not. It's only stone. It doesn't really mean anything."

She knew she must keep telling herself the same story, so that the oracle's ominous words would not alarm her.

At the same time she was beginning to feel happier. Robert had asked her if the oracle had said anything about 'us'. And she was wise enough to know that no man would ask such a question unless the matter of 'us' was important to him.

Now she could hope that he might be hers.

But for how long?

'*I see danger – I see death.*'

She forced the thought away from her, determined not to allow anything to spoil her time of dawning happiness.

When Vanda had said goodnight and retired to her cabin, Robert walked onto the deck and stood looking at the moon overhead. He thought of the moment that he had shared with Vanda in the strange, mysterious temple.

He thought of the Gods who had lived so long ago and yet still seemed to exist now.

Was this just because they were fascinating or because they were real?

Or were they only real to those who believed?

How could anyone know the answer?

He began to be half afraid that his mind was wandering and descended to his own cabin.

Undressing quickly, he climbed into bed and fell asleep.

*

After they had left Itea, the ship began to make its way

to Piraeus, the port from which they would travel to Athens and on to the Parthenon.

Vanda stood at the rail, looking at Greece as they steamed past.

She felt as though the trees, the rocks and the occasional glimpses of stone buildings, all possessed a story to tell her if she could only stop and listen.

It was as though her experience in Delphi had left her mysteriously in tune with the whole country and its amazing history.

Soon after breakfast they moved into the port of Piraeus.

They had laughed and talked during the meal, but Robert could sense that her mind was elsewhere, in Greece, in the past. It was clearly difficult for her to force herself to speak of today when she was really living centuries earlier.

When they were ready to go ashore, he looked at the new hat she had bought in Venice and said,

"You look delightful. You will soon be surrounded by admirers again."

"I do hope not," Vanda stated. "People will seem out of place when all I want to hear is the voice and music of another age."

It was their intention to go straight to the Parthenon, but as they passed through the city of Athens, Vanda looked out at the shops, bright-eyed and eager, until at last Robert grinned and said,

"Shall we indulge in a shopping expedition first?"

"Oh, yes please," she replied at once and he laughed.

Vanda was soon plunged into the fascination of shopping in a foreign land. Above all she was entranced by the pictures.

She also found some music which she was told was

very old. It was sometimes played at a service held on some of the more sacred islands.

She was so thrilled with what she was seeing that her eyes shone and it seemed to Robert that she was now more beautiful than he had ever seen her.

"Look! Look at this!" Vanda kept saying as she found something even more exciting.

He smiled. Her enthusiasm was irresistible.

He even found himself buying ornaments he would certainly not have bought anywhere else. But because they meant so much to Vanda he began to feel that they were important to him too.

'Have I really fallen in love after all this time?' he mused silently. 'And with this woman of all women, who loves to tease and laugh at me and treats me with no respect at all?'

Other women had always treated him carefully because they were trying to lure him on and avoid offending him. But as long as he had known Vanda, she had never seemed to care if she offended him or not. She said exactly what she thought and if he became indignant she only laughed.

Despite this drawback, or perhaps because of it, he had always enjoyed her company, sensing that their minds were often in perfect accord. Their squabbling was simply the communication of people who understood each other well enough to come straight to the point.

'We have pretty much seen the worst of each other,' he thought with an inward grin. 'I have seen her when she has taken a tumble out hunting, sitting up, covered in mud and giving a blistering piece of her mind to the luckless idiot who had caused her fall.

'Then I have seen her jump up and soothe her horse as gently as any mother with a child. I have known her as a damned good sport, a woman any man would like to have as a sister, a comrade.

'And recently I have known her as a creature of beauty and mystery. And suddenly I was jealous. It was as though the final piece had fallen into place.'

Lost in this happy dream, he did not at first realise that someone was trying to attract his attention. But at last he heard the sultry, feminine voice, calling him from a few feet away.

"Robert! Can it possibly be you?"

He turned round and the smile froze on his lips.

"Lady Felicity," he said.

He hoped he did not sound as shocked as he felt. She was the very last person he wanted to see, intruding on this special time with Vanda.

He had known Lady Felicity Janson three years ago, when she was one of the great beauties of London. She had been a widow, not an innocent young girl and they had enjoyed a brief, intense love affair, spending several nights together. He had even wondered if she might be the one woman he was seeking.

But the mood passed. Beautiful as she was, she was also so demanding and authoritative that his passion died. He knew he could never be happy with a woman who tried to boss him.

He had left London sooner than he had intended merely because he was sure his affair with Felicity had gone too far. He discovered that she had started to make enquiries about how rich he was.

He was used to being pursued by women. Most of them were young girls, whose parents made the discreet or not so discreet enquiries.

He had grown to know the calculating looks in their eyes. Although they quivered beneath his kisses, he sensed that their brains were somewhere else, making plans for spending his wealth.

And he wanted nothing to do with them. He had known it then and he knew it more certainly now that he had found his perfect woman.

"Felicity," he stammered again, trying to sound enthusiastic.

"My dear, dear Robert," she said in the breathy, cooing voice that had once enthralled him. "How charming to see you again. Whatever are you doing here? Never mind, you will have plenty of time to tell me now we have been reunited."

"That would be delightful but I am afraid I shall be here only for a few hours. I am on a cruise and the ship departs tomorrow morning."

"But you don't have to depart with it, surely?" she said, putting her head on one side, just as she had done so many times in the days of his infatuation.

It had been charm itself then. Now it warned him that difficult times were ahead.

"I am afraid I do," he said firmly.

"Oh, surely not," she retorted at once. "Nobody will mind if you 'jump ship' to be with me."

"I am afraid my departure date is fixed."

"Nonsense, nonsense," she said gaily.

He remembered now how impossible it was to make her accept anything that did not suit her.

"I am staying with friends in Athens," she babbled on. "Lord and Lady Faine, I think you know them. I will inform them that you are coming to join us."

"But I am not coming to join you," he insisted, beginning to feel as if he was fighting his way through glue.

"Of course you are. I am staying here another week,

and then we can leave and return to England together."

She laid a hand on his arm and looked up into his face with a simper.

"It will be just like old times," she cooed. "We can get to know each other all over again."

It would have been ungallant to say that he already knew far more about her than he wanted to, so Robert merely removed her hand and said stoutly,

"Alas, I must deny myself that pleasure."

"How can you be so unkind?" Lady Felicity asked. "You must know, dearest Robert, that I would rather be with you than anyone else."

"We will meet as soon as I return to England," Robert promised. "But at the moment I am somewhat tied up and it is impossible for me to change my plans."

She was still for a moment. Then she murmured softly,

"You used to change any plan for me. I have never forgotten how happy we were together."

He began to feel both alarmed and trapped. Their last meeting had been three years ago. Yet she had slipped back into a way of talking as though it had been only yesterday.

"Of course we were happy," he agreed. "I look forward to our next meeting at a later date in England."

"That must be not only a promise but a vow," Lady Felicity urged. "Oh, darling, I miss you. I have missed you ever since you ran away and left me in London all alone."

"I imagine there were a dozen men, if not more, to take my place," Robert replied cynically. "Let me just say you are just as beautiful today as you were all that time ago."

"That is what I wanted to hear you say."

"And now I must leave you," he said desperately. "Until another time."

He bowed and hurried quickly away in search of Vanda. He found her examining some small marble figures.

"Look!" she exclaimed. "The faces of the Gods."

Robert's eyes twinkled as he offered,

"I will give them to you, so that you will always remember your first visit to Greece."

"Thank you so much!" Vanda cried. "I will keep them near my bed and talk to them every night."

Her eyes shone as she added,

"I expect that's what they are used to and they would feel lost and forgotten if they were ignored."

"I wonder just how big your collection is by now," he mused, smiling at her

"Oh, dear! Am I being greedy?"

"Of course not, I want you to have everything that you want. Now, why don't we go and look at the Parthenon?"

He arranged for her purchases to be taken directly to the ship and they climbed back into their carriage to complete the journey to the Parthenon.

It would be a relief, he thought, to move away from here, where Felicity might reappear at any moment.

He did not want to have to explain this woman to Vanda. Perhaps later, he thought, when he had made Vanda more securely his own.

He tried to reassure himself that things would work out well. But he had been badly shaken and as they drove away he could not resist looking back, as though afraid that Felicity might be in hot pursuit.

# CHAPTER NINE

The great temple to Athene towers high over the city of Athens. It is a beautiful oblong building, with many tall pillars still standing.

As they travelled towards the temple, Vanda raised her eyes upwards in wonder.

For a while they wandered through the ruins in silence and then Robert murmured,

"I remember Alberto saying that he and Ginetta came here when they first met."

"Yes, they claim it is a temple to love," Vanda said. "And so it is – in a way."

"In a way?"

"It is devoted to Athene, who actually represented spiritual development and understanding," Vanda said. "But surely love is more than emotion, however sweet. Understanding matters too. It is not enough for lovers' hearts to be close. If their minds cannot meet, love cannot last."

"How true that is," he agreed.

Her words made him think of Lady Felicity, whose mind never dwelt on anything but herself, her own appearance, how much money she could grab, how many jewels she could own. He remembered also that she became violently hysterical when she did not get her own way.

She was driven solely by emotion, not sweet, generous emotion, but that of a spoilt, selfish child.

How different was Vanda, in whom heart and mind were perfectly balanced. The ideal woman for now and for the future. For ever.

He could have cursed at the way he had found her only at the moment when their love was threatened by this vulgar interloper.

He tried to reassure himself that all would be well. He had managed to get rid of Felicity before she made a scene, which she would certainly do if she had known about Vanda.

That would surely be the end of the matter?

But he knew in his heart that Felicity was not that easily defeated.

As they climbed into their carriage and drove away, Vanda took one last look at the Parthenon.

"I felt so wonderful here – as though we have been blessed by the Gods."

"I think we were already blessed before we arrived here," he said, "because we escaped something that would have been a disaster?"

She looked at him and he saw her grow pale.

"You mean our marriage?" she said. "Yes, of course – it would have been a disaster."

"No, not our marriage," he replied gently. "But if we had married *under those circumstances,* with your father bullying us, so that we would never had a chance to discover what we really felt. *That* would have been a disaster."

"Oh, yes, of course it would," she answered quickly.

"We should thank whichever Gods protect us that we found the sense to leave and find our own way to – well, our own way."

Vanda nodded. He saw her eyes shining and was

struck by their glory. It seemed to him that Vanda herself looked like a Goddess with her raven black hair and her perfect features.

She might, in fact, have been one of those deities who lived on from generation to generation and was just as lovely today as she had been thousands of years earlier.

"What are you thinking?" she asked.

"Something that would make you laugh if I told you."

"Tell me."

"No, I have no desire to be laughed at."

He would not budge from his position, although he enjoyed Vanda's attempts to tease it out of him.

They arrived back at the ship to find that a party was in progress on deck.

"Nothing like an engagement for a celebration," said a passenger thrusting champagne glasses into their hands.

The happy young couple were Sarah Lake and Myles Dayton, who had been brought on the cruise by their families, both of whom were eager for the match and thought that a romantic atmosphere would help.

"And it did," Sarah bubbled to Vanda. "We nearly became engaged once before, but we were always quarrelling about silly things. Then, when we came here, everything was different."

"It was as though the Gods and Goddesses spoke to us out of the past," Myles added. "And they told us that our ridiculous bickering did not matter. What really mattered was our love."

"But you are so young!" Vanda protested, laughing but also a little dismayed.

Sarah was about seventeen and Myles could not have been more than twenty.

"Too young to know our own minds, you mean?"

Myles said amiably. "But we have the blessing of the Gods, so all will be well."

"Robert, they are no more than children," Vanda commented when they were alone.

"I know. I have been talking to the families, who are both very wealthy and I think they encouraged this romance as a way of merging their fortunes."

"Well – "

"But despite the parents' cynical motives, I cannot help feeling that the match may be right. They adore each other, that's obvious. I suppose the Gods work their magic on the very young as well as – people who have lived only a little. If we are lucky, we all come to the same conclusion in the end."

"You talk about 'the Gods', but I wonder how much you really believe in them, and how much you are humouring me."

"I used not to believe in the Gods," he responded thoughtfully, "but since we have been in Greece – well, did you see what was written on the wall in the temple of Delphi – *Know Thyself*?"

"Yes, I saw it."

"I have come to know myself recently, in all sorts of new and different ways. Haven't you felt that too, about yourself?"

"Yes, I understand things I never even dreamed about before," she said in a low voice. "Things that I never expected to happen – and yet they did. And now I will never be the same again."

He nodded, looking deep into her eyes and she felt a sweet peace come over her. Love came when the time was right.

"There is so much I must say to you," Robert said

softly. "Later – when we are alone. It is time we – we will talk later."

"Yes," she murmured. "Alone."

Somebody sat down at the piano and began to play. He played song after song, while the party fell silent, listening to the sweet, yearning music.

Vanda stood watching the engaged couple, gazing into each other's eyes, sensing the feelings that inspired them and longing for the moment when she too could confess her love.

She felt a sudden need to be alone and wandered a little way off to stand by the rail, looking out over the sea on which the moon was shining.

Watching her from a distance, Robert thought she looked as though she had found her way to Heaven while still on earth.

'What she is really seeking,' he told himself, is '*the world beyond the world*'. Yes, these are the right words to describe her goal.'

He had not considered such an idea before.

It seemed to him very strange and not in the least like himself to be thinking in such a way.

But he knew this was what Vanda was thinking and feeling, even though perhaps she could not put it into words.

'She is unique,' he thought to himself, 'and there is no one like her. But what about me? Will she let me into her '*world beyond the world*?' Or will she shut me out forever? How strange! I thought I knew her so well, but now I cannot predict anything about her.'

Around him the party was breaking up. People were drifting off to bed.

He became aware that a Steward was at his elbow, murmuring,

"A lady to see you, my Lord!"

He looked round in surprise.

Then, to his shock and horror, he could see Lady Felicity approaching.

She was dressed to be noticed, in a deep red velvet evening gown with a plunging neckline. Around her neck was a heavy ruby and gold necklace.

Except that they were decidedly not rubies, he realised. They were fakes. He was certain he was right because he had seen her wearing the original necklace and this imitation was not quite perfect.

She must have spent most of her fortune and was now desperate for another.

"Dearest Robert," she announced, enveloping him in a scented embrace. "I could not let you go without seeing you again. It was so unexpected that you should be here in this outlandish place that for the moment my brain was not working. I should have asked you to dinner or visited you here for dinner with you."

"How do you come to be here?" he asked.

"It wasn't easy to find you," she replied in a teasing voice, "since you forgot to give me the name of your ship. But you said you were departing tomorrow and this was the only vessel in port that leaves tomorrow."

So she had expended a considerable amount of time and energy tracking him down, he thought grimly.

"So I thought I would give you a lovely surprise," she continued.

"How charming of you!" he said in a thin voice. "I had not expect – er – hoped to see you again."

"But my darling, I have so many wonderful memories – as I know you do."

"Delightful memories," he responded untruthfully. "But those days are past."

"Not in my heart," she said huskily. "Sometimes I lie awake and think of the nights we spent together. I know that I could never know such love-making with any other man, just as you could never know it with any other woman."

"You rate my prowess too highly," he countered.

She gave a throaty chuckle.

"Oh, you naughty man!"

Robert ground his teeth at being called a 'naughty man'. Her childish talk had irked him even when he was infatuated by her physical charms. Now it nauseated him.

"I meant the way our hearts beat as one," she purred. "I was not just talking about your prowess – although that was considerable. I cannot wait to experience you again."

It was like moving through a nightmare. The only bright spot was the fact that she plainly did not realise that Vanda was with him.

There was an expression in her eyes and the way her hand clasped his, which made Robert realise she was waiting for him to kiss her.

"This is hardly the time or place," he murmured, suppressing a strong desire to pick Felicity up and toss her overboard.

"I remember when anywhere was the right time and place, darling. Why don't we go to your cabin now and remind ourselves of old times. Then we can pack your trunks and leave."

For a moment Robert could not think what he could do. His mind was a terrifying blank.

Then as Felicity moved even nearer to him and raised her hand to touch his cheek again, he said quickly,

"What can I get you to drink? If I remember rightly you prefer champagne to anything else."

He moved determinedly away from her as he spoke.

"Champagne is what we both need," he blurted out with determined cheerfulness. "The Steward seems to have disappeared. I will go and find him."

He fled.

Lady Felicity sat down, showing every sign of taking root. She had been put off earlier in the day and she was not going to let it happen again.

From her position further along the deck, Vanda watched, feeling herself turning to stone. She had seen everything from the moment this strange woman with the ripe, exotic beauty had swept onto the ship.

She was a woman of the world. That much was obvious. And from the way she faced Robert and pressed herself against him, looking up intimately into his face, it was also obvious what their relationship had been.

Powerful, agonising jealousy possessed her. She wanted to scream aloud from the force of it. He was *hers*.

But he had never actually said so.

All the times when she had felt certain they were growing closer, they might have been only in her imagination. For the brutal truth was that he had never committed himself.

Even tonight, when he had said they must talk alone – she had thought that he intended to declare his love. But suppose he wanted only to tell her that this journey had gone far enough? That he loved another woman?

How did this painted creature come to be aboard? Had Robert expected her? Invited her?

Vanda turned cold at the thought that he might have actually sent for her to help detach him from herself.

She could bear this suspense no longer. She must discover the truth or go mad.

Determinedly she walked along the deck to where the

stranger was sitting. She looked up and scrutinised Vanda out of huge, dark eyes that might have been beautiful but for their hard, calculating look.

Vanda forced herself to speak normally.

"I am wondering where Lord Cunningham might be. He was here when I left and he didn't mention going to bed."

Lady Felicity's eyes narrowed in astonishment and anger as she realised that this beautiful young woman and Robert must know each other.

"Dear Robert has gone to fetch me some champagne," she replied coldly. "I am afraid I do not have the pleasure of knowing who you are, as he did not mention you to me. Did you meet on this boat?"

Confronted by a straight question, Vanda realised that she should have prepared for this encounter a little more carefully. Now she wondered frantically what she should say. Something was warning her to go carefully. The 'sister' story might be unwise.

"The fact is – " she began slowly.

"Yes, do tell me all about yourself. What is your name?"

"Vanda Sudbury."

"Miss?"

"Yes."

There was a pause during which the woman drummed her elegant fingers on the table.

"Then no doubt your chaperone is somewhere about?" she questioned in a tense voice.

It was clear, from the way she spoke and from the expression in her eyes, what she was thinking.

After a moment when she realised that she was waiting, Vanda said,

"We are related through my grandmother. As we have known each other for many years, Robert thought we might visit some of his relations who had been very fond of my parents. We have just arrived from Italy where we spent a short time with our relatives."

"So you are related?"

"Yes," Vanda replied. "Of course, as we have grown up together, the Earl is like a brother to me."

"Ah, yes, I do recall him mentioning some poor relation or other. My name is Lady Felicity Janson. Robert and I are old and very, very dear friends. I expect he has told you all about me. Our closeness has been such that – well, I am afraid he isn't always very discreet."

"Indeed?" Vanda said politely, although inwardly she was seething.

Pain and anger seemed to rend her apart, but she forced herself to stay still and listen. She wanted to hear everything this woman had to say.

"When we discovered how deeply we felt about each other," Felicity continued, "my husband had not been dead for very long. We needed to be discreet to avoid a scandal."

"You mean people might have thought you did not love your husband?" Vanda asked bluntly.

"Oh, my dear, I was a child when I married. I knew nothing. My parents arranged the match. I was a dutiful wife, but I did not discover love – real, true love – until Robert came into my life."

She paused and a little smile crept over her face. It suggested hot passionate memories, and Vanda, even while she recognised the play acting, clenched her fists out of sight. Otherwise she might have tried to scratch Felicity's eyes out.

"Oh, what a discovery that was!" Felicity persisted. "To have been a wife in a cold, loveless marriage and then to have passion revealed in one overwhelming experience! How can I describe it? How can I find the words?"

'*I am sure you will manage it,*' Vanda thought grimly.

"I will never forget that first night," Felicity sighed. "How we approached each other, trembling with passion, uncertain into what shoals our love would lead us. And next – the revelation that we were destined for each other."

"But you never announced your engagement?" Vanda enquired sweetly.

"Not then. It was necessary to allow a little time to elapse for the sake of propriety. If you could only understand the agony of keeping such a great love a secret. To look at each other across the room and know the truth, yet still have to talk to other people."

She gave Vanda a smile, evidently intended to be sympathetic, but which managed to be only hard.

"My dear, I do hope that one day you too will know a great love like ours."

"But surely, very few women could know a love exactly like yours," Vanda said.

She counted on Felicity being too stupid to appreciate the double meaning. And she was right.

"How true that is!" Felicity sighed. "We were slaves to our passion and since that time we have thought only of the day when we could be together."

She turned huge, luminous eyes on Vanda.

"I am sure you understand," she murmured.

"Oh, yes, madam," Vanda said. "I understand perfectly."

For a moment a frisson of alarm flickered over Lady Felicity's face, as though she was wondering if any young woman could be quite as guileless as this one seemed to be.

At that moment Robert returned, checking himself

sharply when he found the two of them talking.

There was a thunderstruck pause, during which both women tried to read his face.

Lady Felicity said,

"I was just hearing, Robert, how you are related to this pretty girl. Even so it seems strange that you have not brought a chaperone."

"I have explained," Vanda interjected quickly, "that we are distantly related and that you have been *almost like a brother* to me."

He nodded, picking up her cue.

"We started off with a companion," he said, "but unfortunately she was taken ill when we visited France, so we are picking her up in a day or so when she should have recovered."

Lady Felicity who had been frowning, smiled.

"So you do not have a chaperone at this moment?" she queried.

"We do not really need one," Robert answered. "I have known Vanda ever since she was born and we have always felt as if we were brother and sister."

Brother and sister.

To Vanda the message was clear. He was telling her that their relationship was once more on the old footing. There was nothing else.

She could endure no more. She forced her stiff body to rise and move away along the deck. She knew if she was sensible she would go below, but she could not bear to let them out of her sight.

Yet she must go where she could not hear them.

Robert, glancing up, discovered that Vanda was no longer present. She had moved so softly and so quietly that he had not seen her depart.

A suffocating feeling came over him at the realisation that he was now alone with Felicity.

"So she is your relative," Felicity reflected. "Therefore there is no reason for me to be jealous?"

To Robert's relief the Steward arrived with the champagne, which he poured and departed.

"Now tell me, dearest," Felicity said when they were alone, "have you missed me while we have been apart? Do you want me to say how lonely and miserable I have been without you?"

He could endure no more. Putting down his glass of champagne he said,

"Forgive me, but I must speak to Vanda."

He did not wait for Felicity to reply, but slipped out through the door. Hurrying down the deck, he found Vanda a little further on, just out of sight of Felicity, leaning over the rail.

As he moved beside her she looked up at him and asked,

"You are neglecting your visitor?"

"Then she can leave," he replied sharply. "But for reasons I cannot explain to you now, I do not wish to be alone with her. Will you come back and chaperone me?"

*"What?"*

"We have to make her believe – anything that will get rid of her."

"Such as?"

"I don't know. We can think up a good story."

"She looks as though she would be suspicious of anything."

"I will just have to make her believe me."

"How?" Vanda asked.

"By lying, of course," he said bluntly. "I am good at it. I learnt at school and I have been lying ever since."

"Really? I have always believed that you told the truth, the whole truth and nothing but the truth."

"Nonsense, you have never believed any such thing," he snapped.

"I was being polite," she snapped back.

"Will you help me get rid of her?"

Vanda gave a brittle laugh.

"She is your friend, not mine," she said. "But perhaps 'friend' is the wrong word."

*"Meaning?"*

"You surely don't need me to explain? I didn't think you were so naïve. Well, it's like this. When a man – "

"All right, all right," he said hastily.

"Good. I was sure you were too experienced to need explanations."

"I am not experienced enough to cope with *her*," he said desperately. "I don't believe that any man is."

"You speak from knowledge, of course."

"If you mean was she my mistress once, *yes* she was," he screamed, goaded beyond endurance. "Does it matter? You knew I had mistresses. You said so. I remember you seemed to find it a very good joke."

"My dear Robert," she asserted coolly, "it is nothing to me whether you have one mistress or a thousand, as long as you do not bring any of them on this journey."

"Do you seriously imagine that I want her here?"

"I don't know. Tell me."

"You shouldn't need telling. Have the last few days meant nothing to you? I thought we understood each other – "

"So did I."

"Then we were both wrong, because if we had, you would not be asking me this kind of tom fool question. I want that woman out of here and I need your help."

"Why? Just throw her out."

"That is easier said than done. She is the sort of woman who always has her own way. If you had seen one of her tearful rages you would understand. If we are not careful she will join this ship. Do you want that?"

"I thought I was being tactful in keeping away."

"Oh, did you!" he replied wrathfully. "Look, it was years ago, and we were definitely not as close as she likes to think."

"Really?" she responded in a withering voice. "Well, it's fairly obvious *what she thinks.*"

He ground his teeth.

"Could we discuss this later?"

"I am perfectly happy to discuss it now."

"I think that's rather indelicate of you."

"Well, I think it is rather indelicate of you to bring your mistress on our trip."

"She is not my mistress. Not any more."

"She would like to be, though."

"That is what I am asking you to help me prevent, but you are being very stupid about it!"

"Thank you!"

"Don't mention it."

After a frozen silence he said,

"I suppose I should be glad that you *are* jealous."

"How dare you say I am jealous!"

"Well, I was jealous of you when you carried on with Piero in Paris. If I can admit it, why can't you?"

"You never did admit it."

"I have just admitted it now. I will say it again. I was jealous, *I was jealous.* Is that clear enough?"

She stared at him while her heart began to soar.

"Do you mean that?"

"Good Lord, Vanda, you do pick some strange times to ask silly questions! Yes, I mean it. I am in love with you. I have probably been in love with you for a long time but I could not see it.

"Well, I have seen it now and you are going to listen to me whether you want to or not. I love you. I want to marry you, and I am *going* to marry you, even if you are the most exasperating woman on earth. So what have you got to say about that?"

# CHAPTER TEN

"What – what did you say?" Vanda whispered.

"I said you are the most exasperating woman on earth."

"No – the bit before that."

"I said I am going to marry you. We have shilly-shallied long enough and now it's settled. We are getting married and that's that – unless you have some objection."

The stars seemed to reel in the Heavens as the full impact of his words dawned on her.

"No," she sighed, breathless with joy. "I have no objection."

The next moment his arms tightened around her. Vanda felt herself pulled hard against him as his mouth descended on hers.

Now she was in Heaven, kissing the man she loved, feeling him kiss her with all his heart and soul.

"My darling Vanda," he murmured against her lips. "I must have loved you a long, long time without knowing."

"And I – " she said happily, "I thought I only cared for you as a brother. How could I be so wrong?"

"Kiss me," he urged hoarsely. "Kiss me and tell me that this is really happening and not some dream. I don't want to wake up."

"We will never wake up," Vanda breathed.

"Tell me that you love me."

"I love you, I love you. I always will."

"And I will always love you," he vowed.

He kissed her again. In her riot of happiness she felt her last fear slip away. The oracle had been wrong to predict danger and death. There had been this happiness in store for them all the time.

*"No!"*

A scream of rage and anguish shattered their moment, forcing them to pull apart and turn to see Lady Felicity running along the deck towards them.

*"No!"* she screamed again. "Robert, how can you do this to me? You love *me*."

"I do *not* love you, Felicity. I love Vanda and she is going to be my wife."

"You are lying," she cried, hysterical tears pouring down her face. "You love me. You know you do."

"Felicity, stop this scene," Robert ordered, coming forward to confront her. "I don't love you, and you don't really love me."

"I do, I love you," she shrieked. "I won't let anyone else have you. *I mean it.*"

Before either of them realised what she was doing, Felicity plunged her hand into her purse and drew out a tiny revolver.

"I won't let her have you," she screamed. "Do you understand that?"

"Felicity – " Robert said, closing in on her slowly, "give me that gun."

"Stay where you are." She waved the revolver at him. "Send her away, Robert. You don't love her, you love me."

There was a roaring in Vanda's ears. Suddenly she was back in Delphi, hearing the oracle predict blood and death.

And her own reply,

"*Who will die? Not him, I beg you. Take me, not him.*"

Suddenly Lady Felicity raised her arm.

"*Take me, not him.*"

In a terrifying jumble of sounds Vanda heard herself scream and Robert's howl of anguish as the revolver exploded.

Everything was confusion. The gun, though tiny, had seemed to bellow. Vanda saw the flash of the explosion against the darkness, then she was on the ground hearing hurrying footsteps, women screaming and men shouting.

She was surrounded by people. Arms reached out to help her into a sitting position and she realised that Felicity's bullet had missed her. Apart from a few bruises she was uninjured. Helped by willing hands she climbed to her feet.

"Are you hurt?" someone asked.

"No," she gasped, "but Robert – ?"

She looked around frantically, crying,

"Where is he?"

A man's voice said,

"He is hurt. The bullet caught him."

"Oh, no – no."

Suddenly she saw Robert lying on the deck, an ugly red stain upon his shirt.

"That woman tried to shoot you." It was Sarah, the bride whose engagement had prompted the party. "But he pushed you out of the way and took the bullet himself."

"What did you say?" Vanda whispered in horror.

"We heard her screaming and ran to see what the noise

145

was about. We were just in time to see her fire the revolver."

"She was aiming for you," said Myles, who was beside his fiancée. "She would have shot you because it was only a few feet. But he yelled *'no'* and shoved you aside so hard that you fell and he was right in the line of fire."

"The Captain has ordered her to be taken below and locked up," Sarah added.

"I must see Robert," she cried. "Oh, dear God, don't let him die."

She ran frantically across the deck to where Robert lay, frighteningly still and white.

"Robert," she wept flinging herself down beside him, "*Robert!*"

But he did not move. His eyes were closed and his breathing was shallow.

"He needs a doctor," she screamed.

"I am afraid this ship is too small to carry a doctor," said the Captain worriedly. "We will have to find one in the locality."

"But that could take hours," she cried.

She touched Robert's face while tears streamed down her face.

"No," she whispered, "please not now, when we have just found each other. Oh, God, please help!"

She closed her eyes and prayed frantically.

'Send him a doctor now, this minute. He cannot afford to wait.'

She did not know exactly which deity she was addressing. Was it the God she had always known? Or was it one – or all – of the ancient deities that had once ruled this country and, in many ways, still did?

Whatever the answer – and perhaps it was both – she cried out inwardly to the presence she had felt at Delphi.

"I asked you to take *me*, not *him*. Why didn't you listen?"

There was no reply, only a profound silence. But in the midst of it, she felt a sense of reproach, as though someone had said –

"*Be patient. All is not yet ended.*"

'Save him,' she prayed. 'Save him.'

"Stand back please. Let me get to him."

Startled, she looked up to see a man, whom she recognised as one of the passengers, bustling through the crowd in a purposeful manner. He was in a dressing gown and looked as though he had just been roused from his bed.

He took charge, brooking no argument and brushing everyone else aside.

"He needs a doctor," Vanda cried.

"I *am* a doctor, madam," he said crisply. "I am Sir Steven Tranley, Chief General Surgeon at the Victoria Hospital in London."

Vanda's hands flew to her mouth. She had heard of Sir Steven, a brilliant surgeon, knighted for his services to the Royal family the previous year.

A young boy helped her to her feet.

"My father never tells people he is a doctor when we are on holiday," he told her quietly. "But this was an emergency, so I fetched him."

"Oh, thank you, thank you," she wept.

Men were lifting Robert and carrying him below. She followed them down to his cabin, where a Steward tried to bar her way.

"This is no sight for a lady," he ventured.

"My place is with him," Vanda demanded emphatically. "Kindly get out of my way or I shall be forced to knock you down."

The Steward backed off hurriedly.

Vanda approached the bed, terrified at what she would see.

Sir Steven had removed Robert's shirt, revealing blood pouring from a wound in his shoulder.

Vanda fought back a feeling of sickness. She must not give way to weakness. Robert needed her.

"I cannot afford females in here, having the vapours," Sir Steven said brusquely.

"I shall not have the vapours," Vanda informed him. "I can do whatever is needed."

From the bed came an incredible sound. Robert's eyes were open and he had actually managed a faint laugh.

"That's my girl," he croaked hoarsely.

"Robert," she whispered. "Oh, thank God, you are awake!"

"Are you all right, my darling?"

"Yes, I am not hurt."

"Then all is well."

His words finished in a groan as the doctor began to work on him.

"I am going to have to dig that bullet out," Sir Steven grunted.

"He is going to survive, isn't he?" Vanda pleaded.

"If the bullet hasn't touched the lung he will be all right. If it has – "

He left the implication hanging in the air.

His son had been sent to fetch his black bag. From it the doctor took a small bottle and sprinkled a few drops onto a clean handkerchief.

"Lay this over his face," he instructed Vanda. "Do not come too close or you will breathe it in yourself."

"I don't want that stuff," Robert whispered. "I hate the idea of being unconscious."

"You will hate the pain even more," the doctor stated.

Vanda took the handkerchief.

"Trust me," she told Robert, and saw him relax at once.

The next moment she placed the linen over his face and watched as his eyes closed.

She was glad she had done so, when she saw the doctor at work, digging for the bullet. How could any man have endured the pain, she thought?

At last Sir Steven drew out the bullet and held it up.

"Here it is," he called triumphantly.

"His lung – ?"

"Just missed it. He was lucky. It was a very close call."

"Thank God!" she murmured.

"Never mind that," Sir Steven said caustically. "There is still work to be done. I am going to bind up his wound and then I am returning to bed."

He was far from being the most agreeable man Vanda had ever met, but she could see now how he had acquired his reputation as a brilliant surgeon. He bandaged up the wound efficiently and gave his instructions in a brusque voice.

"He will probably develop a fever and become restless. If so, give him some of this," he said, placing a small vial by the bed. "Now I am going to bed."

"But he is safe now?" she implored, longing to hear him say the words. "The bullet missed his lung so he is not going to die?"

"I cannot say that. I have done all I can and for the rest you will have to be patient. Goodnight."

He was gone and she was alone with the sleeping Robert. To her relief she noticed that his colour was better, but she knew that he could still be in danger.

The bullet had not touched his lung. She must cling to that thought.

Now she had time to think over what she had been told – that he had saved her at the cost of being shot himself.

*She had been ready to die for him and it seemed that he had been ready to die for her.*

As the minutes and the hours glided past, she had plenty of time to reflect.

Each would have died for the other.

He stirred and she leaned closer, watching until his eyes opened.

"Is that you?" he murmured.

"Yes, my darling, I am here with you. I will always be here."

"Yes, you must always be here, for I cannot live without you."

She took his hand, holding it gently.

"Kiss me," he said.

Slowly she leaned forward and pressed her lips lovingly against his. As she drew back she saw his eyes closing again.

She sat quietly beside him, allowing him the sleep he needed, while inwardly she spoke to an unseen presence that she knew was with her.

'*This was what you tried to tell me – blood and danger. And death? But there will be no death. I will not permit it. He is mine and I am going to keep him safe.*'

The ancient Greeks had believed that when a man died he went to the ferry that crossed the River Styx and handed a coin to the ferryman whose name was Charon, and he took the dead man across the river to Hades, the underworld.

Now Vanda sat holding onto Robert's hands, as if by doing so she could hold him back from the ferry. There would be no coin, she vowed, and no voyage across the Styx. The ferryman could wait forever. While she possessed the strength to fight him, he would leave without his passenger.

She felt her head droop and forced herself to raise it. Now that the agitation of the evening was over, she could feel weariness overtaking her. Her eyelids drooped.

She jerked up again. Robert's hands were hot in hers and he was growing restless.

Quickly she poured some drops into the glass and supported him with her arm while he drank. To her relief he grew quieter.

It seemed to her that now he slept more deeply and she became afraid lest his sleep grew too deep and he never awakened.

She leaned close again, watching his face intently, looking for any signs of change. But suddenly it was dark and she could not see him properly.

The air was cold and a chill wind whistled about her face. A dank miasma came off the water and the man in the ferry was drawing nearer. He was standing upright, driving his boat along with one huge oar.

At the water's edge he stopped and held out his hand.

"No," Vanda cried firmly.

He neither moved nor spoke, but stood holding his hand out with terrible patience. She tried to outface him but it was hard when she could not see his eyes. The hood of his great cloak hung low, obscuring his face.

"Go," she told him. "There is nothing for you here."

Silence. Only that motionless figure, the hand

outstretched to eternity.

Robert's breathing was growing shallow. There were dark circles around his eyes and his skin was grey.

It was now or never.

She gathered her courage and stepped forward, flinging her arm wide so that the ferryman's hand was knocked aside.

*"You shall not take him!"*

In that instant the cloak collapsed, revealing that there was nothing beneath. The waters opened, swallowing up the boat and the darkness vanished.

Vanda opened her eyes to find that she was lying on the bed beside Robert. It was morning and the room was flooded with light.

Best of all, his eyes were open and he was looking at her fondly.

"Are you all right?" he asked. "You were talking in your sleep, but I couldn't make out the words."

Joyfully she felt his forehead.

"Your fever has gone," she said. "You are going to recover."

"Yes, I am. I can feel it now. And you have been with me all night, haven't you?"

"Every moment, my love. I did not dare to leave you."

"You stayed to fight the battle with me."

"We fought it together."

"I felt you. It was as though a tide was trying to carry me on, but you were holding me against your heart and I knew that as long as you held me, I was safe."

Then he frowned as though trying to remember something and asked,

"Who is Charon, my darling?"

"Charon?"

"Yes, when I awoke you were lying with your arm over me, murmuring in your sleep."

Dazed, she sat up and tried to think.

"Did I actually say his name? I don't remember that. I only remember that he had no face."

"But who is he?"

"Later, my love."

There would be a time to discuss these mysteries with him, but it was not now.

They could hear the ship coming to life around them. Vanda hastily slid off the bed as the doctor returned, bringing with him the Captain.

It was soon clear to everyone that the danger was past and Robert needed only rest and good nursing.

But the Captain had another worry.

"What should be done with the woman who shot you?" he asked Robert. "If you wish me to hand her over to the police, of course I will but – "

He finished with a helpless gesture that spoke volumes about the horror of having to drag the passengers back to be witnesses in a trial. Or worse still, having them detained in Greece indefinitely.

"There is no need for that," Robert said. "Send for the British Consul and release her to him. Then let us set sail."

"Thank you, my Lord," said the Captain gratefully.

Vanda had slipped out of the cabin and gone to stand on deck, looking out over the water, sparkling in the early morning sun. She stood there until the brilliant light had driven the last of the darkness away.

Only she knew how different it might have been.

They had been together during that long night and they

had emerged victorious together because their love was eternal.

Then she grew suddenly still at something she thought she saw on the horizon. The harbour was crowded with boats, large and small, and there was no chance that she could distinguish one from another. And yet –

And yet –

Far off she seemed to make out one small boat, with a tall figure standing in it, motionless.

"Charon," she whispered. "Perhaps there are more battles to be fought in the times ahead, but however often you return for him, I shall be there to fight you away.

"I want long years with him, many children and grandchildren. But be patient. One day we will climb into your ferry together, and you can take us both across the Styx to that other world where we will never be parted."

The sun flashed, forcing her to close her eyes. When she opened them again, Charon and his ferry had gone.

She stayed on deck until the British Consul arrived and went below. A few moments later he re-appeared with Felicity, who cast Vanda a look of hatred, before lifting her chin and marching haughtily ashore.

At once the ship sprang into feverish life. Everyone was anxious to sail away quickly.

Vanda returned to Robert's cabin just as Sir Steven was leaving.

"Everything is fine," he announced testily. "I have dressed the wound again and there is no sign of infection. He should make a full recovery. Now, if nobody minds, I would like continue with my holiday."

He stalked away in high dudgeon.

Vanda slipped into Robert's cabin to find him sitting up in bed, his eyes bright with health. He raised his good arm to her and she joined him on the bed.

She moved carefully so as not to injure him, but at once he tightened his arm about her and she could feel his renewed strength.

Then he was kissing her and his kisses were full of vigour and life.

She felt her heart give itself to Robert forever, knowing that she would never want anything or anyone but him and his love.

"We will travel straight home," he said, "and marry as soon as possible. And then we can never be parted again."

He kissed her and she put her arms about his neck, returning his kisses with fervour.

"How could we have been so long together without discovering our love?" he murmured.

"We discovered it when the time was right," she insisted. "We needed to be friends and companions first and that will always be part of our love."

"Yes. Now I know why no other woman ever satisfied me completely. They all lacked that extra 'something' that I only found in you and which will satisfy and fulfil me all my life."

His brow darkened as he added,

"When I saw that woman aim at your heart, I knew that if she killed you, my own life would be over."

"But I feel the same," she said passionately. "My life is nothing without you."

He did not reply in words, but he nodded, his eyes meeting hers in perfect communion.

Not only their hearts but their minds were as one, and their union would be strong for all eternity.

"I ask nothing but to be with you," he said. "Love me, my darling, for now I have found you and I know I can never do without you again. Promise to stay with me forever."

"Forever," Vanda agreed. "And beyond."

"And beyond," he repeated. "Then we shall have everything – perfect happiness, perfect ecstasy, perfect love."

She nestled into his arms with a sigh of deep contentment.

The ship had started to move. They could feel it thrumming as it glided out of the port towards the horizon, towards the light, towards the future.